DRUNK ON SPORTS

by

TIM COWLISHAW

Foreword
by
Charles Barkley

Vigliano Books

DRUNK ON SPORTS

Cover design by ExpertSubjects.com

Published by Vigliano Books
http://www.viglianoassociates.com

Digital design by Telemachus Press, LLC
http://www.telemachuspress.com

ISBN# 978-0-9893300-0-8 (paperback)

Version 2013.05.31

Printed in the United States of America

10 9 8 7 6 5 4 3 2 1

To Willis

He taught me what every good father should teach his son:

The love of good books and the proper use of the mulligan.

CONTENTS

DRUNK ON SPORTS

PRELUDE

TEXAS DEPARTMENT OF PUBLIC SAFETY OFFENSE
REPORT
DATE: July 21, 2007
TIME: 3:18 A.M.
COUNTY: Hunt.
PLACE: I-30 SFR, E of FM 1565.

SYNOPSIS: On 7-21-2007, I stopped a vehicle for driving on
the wrong side of the road. Upon contact with the vehicle a
strong odor of alcoholic beverage was detected. I got the
driver out of the vehicle and detected an odor of alcohol
coming from him. When I asked the driver if he had anything to drink, he said some beers. After performing SFST's
the driver was arrested for DWI. The driver was transported to Hunt County Jail and released to jailers on duty.

DETAILS

1. I, James Ammons, am a commissioned peace officer in
   the State of Texas employed by the Texas Department of
   Public Safety as a State Trooper in the Texas Highway
   Patrol Service.

2. I was working a STEP shift of 3 am-7 am.

3. I was in a marked black and white car.

4. I had stopped at a sign at the intersection of FM1565N and the Interstate 30 South Frontage Road preparing to turn left onto the SFR when I observed a vehicle traveling east on the SFR that had stopped on the shoulder of the SFR right in front of me. I observed the driver moving around in the vehicle. The driver then looked in my direction, put his seat belt on and pulled back on to the south frontage road. I then turned left behind the vehicle. I then observed the vehicle drift into the west bound lane of the SFR traveling east and then continued on the wrong side of the road.

5. I immediately got in behind the vehicle and activated my emergency overhead lights to initiate a traffic stop.

6. The vehicle, a black Toyota Highlander (sport utility) bearing Texas Registration 704-XYT stopped partially on the road and partially on the shoulder of the SFR East of FM 1565.

7. I made a driver side approach and as I approached I detected the strong odor of an alcoholic beverage coming from the vehicle.

8. I identified myself and told the driver my reason for the stop.

9. The driver stated "I know" and said something else but his speech was slurred and I could not understand what he said.

10. At this point I also observed that the driver's eyes were blood shot and glassy.

11. Before I asked the driver for his driver's license and insurance he gave it to me.

12. The driver was identified as Cowlishaw, William Timothy by his Texas Driver's License.

13. I asked Cowlishaw where he was headed and he said home. His driver's license showed a Coppell address which if that is where he still lived he was going in the wrong direction. I asked the driver where he lived and he said Coppell.

FOREWORD

by
Charles Barkley

IT WAS THE spring of 2006 and the TNT crew was on its way to Dallas for the Western Conference Finals when I gave the producers an unusual request. I told them I wanted to meet Tim Cowlishaw.

I don't usually go out of my way to meet members of the media. As a player, I used to have friends in the press. But the media in today's 24-7 news cycle is always trying to get somebody, trying to bring someone down. And I pay very close attention.

I watch *Around the Horn* all the time and, unlike some people on that show, I feel like Tim always tries to play fair. I don't agree with everything he says, but he doesn't have an agenda where he's out to get some people he doesn't like or protect people that he likes. And, you know, I take television and newspapers very seriously. People see something on television or they read it in the newspaper and they think it's gospel.

There are some writers that I have known for years. Michael Wilbon of the *Washington Post*—well, he used to be at the *Post*, now he's on TV more than I am—and David Dupree who was at *USA Today* and Bob Ford at the *Philadelphia Inquirer*. These are great friends. These are all nice guys and they have something in common. They just want to do their job. They're not operating with hidden agendas.

Being fair is all I try to do on TNT. Guys have gotten mad at me. Kobe got mad at me after that playoff game in 2006 when he wouldn't shoot in the second half. He texted me like 100 times, called me every name in the book. I said, "First of all, I've called you the best player in the world for the last three years and you didn't exactly call and thank me. But I didn't like what you did. And I knew what you were doing."

I had never seen Tim trying to go after someone he didn't seem to like or protect someone who's his friend. So I was in Dallas in 2006 at one of my favorite steakhouses, Nick and Sam's. I was talking to some people at the bar and Tim happened to be there. He came walking up to introduce himself but before he could do that, I told him, "Dude, I really appreciate what you do on ESPN because you're fair."

I was leaving the bar when I spoke to him that night, but we met for drinks a lot over the next two years. When I came to Dallas—I was taping the golf show with Hank Haney there that next summer—I would text Tim and we would go out.

We went out drinking in Scottsdale, too, when he was in town for a Cowboys-Cardinals game.

And we went out in LA. And we went out in New York. We drank a lot of beers and more than a few vodka-and-cranberries. It was like it used to be when I was a player, just friends out drinking. Back in the '80s, we would go to the hotel bar and run into the Philly writers there. Now I don't think you can do that anymore. If you don't play well, it would be "Charles was out drinking last night" all over the news.

I think Tim's job is tougher than mine. When you're a local guy, fans want you to say 100 percent positive things about the team all the time. How can he do that? When's the last time the Cowboys were really good? I can't even tell you.

Besides our honesty and our love of sports, Tim and I have one other thing in common. We both got arrested for DWI in recent years. His didn't quite make the big news that mine did. I know he's grateful for that, but I applaud him for telling his story here.

Mine took place on New Year's Eve, 2008. I have a big party in Scottsdale every year and we were leaving the bar. There were three or four cars in a line and I was the fourth car. We all slow-rolled through a stop sign and when I did it, the flashing lights came on and the cop cars came out of the woodwork.

I did a sobriety test, walking the line and all that stuff, and I thought I did pretty good. The cop said, "You did all right." At that point, I knew I was going to jail.

The thing that bothered me was I wasn't driving down the highway weaving or out of control. I rolled through a stop sign. But there were times I'd been driving where I was worse; I know that for sure.

When I had to spend a weekend in jail due to the laws in Arizona, I was just mad at myself. I couldn't believe I fucked up like that. I had never thought about drinking and driving until I got arrested. I never thought about the consequences. And I wasn't even drunk that night; I've been much worse behind the wheel of a car. I'm not bragging about this by any means, but I've had cops follow me home before to make sure I got there OK.

The other thing that really bothered me was how the "blow job" story made national news. That was 100 percent a joke. People think I told the officer who pulled me over that I was in a hurry to get a blow job. I said that three hours later when I had already posted bail and was waiting on a ride. I was just joking around with the officers there who treated me great, by the way. But someone decided to put it in the report and so everyone thinks I said it seriously to get out of the arrest.

But I did learn my lesson. Even though I usually took taxis or hired drivers before, I do it all the time now.

I do find it ironic that the same people who were slamming me, crucifying me or wanting me to get fired are the same people who are fine with the selling of alcoholic beverages at sporting events. I said, wait a minute, I admit that I was wrong here. But you depend on alcohol sales at sporting events, you let people tailgate for hours in your parking lots at NFL games and drive home drunk, so don't play God over me. I accept the fact that I screwed up. But don't make me out to be the worst person in the world unless you are willing to cut off alcohol sales at sporting events.

It was a couple of months after my DWI that I met Tim at one of my favorite places in Dallas called Primo's. He told me that night how he had been arrested for DWI a year or so earlier and how he had kept it quiet but that he wondered if there wasn't something the two of us could do to speak to people with drinking problems.

We didn't figure it out that night. It was maybe a year later that Tim told me he had gone through a lot more than a DWI, that alcohol had nearly killed him and that he had stopped drinking. He told me a little about what he wanted to say in this book and asked if I would write the foreword since our relationship, even though it was based on sports, had been developed by meeting up in bars.

He said there is this bond between sports and drinking that's unlike anything else. People don't get hammered when they go see a movie. They might drink at home while watching their favorite TV show but, for the most part, they don't gather in one public spot to watch it and get drunk.

I've always liked what Tim has to say about sports but, after what he has been through, I admire what he has to say about drinking. It's a lot like what I think about social media.

When we got together in Atlanta in April, 2012 for the foreword of this book, Tim kidded me about still not being on twitter. I told him you just can't make mental mistakes when you're famous. You can't joke on twitter. You can't get mad at people on twitter.

I said, "Let me limit the amount of times shit can happen to me."

That's how Tim looks at drinking now. He told me, 'Drinking is something people do; it's not what you are. But when it becomes what you are, you need to think about becoming something else.'

In this book, he's as honest about his drinking as he has always been about sports and I appreciate him for that.

INTRODUCTION

.266

FOR MOST OF my life, that's looked like a batting average to me. Maybe during my three-year run as a hockey beat writer, I would see that figure and think of a really, really efficient power play. But for most of my first 50 years—starting at age six while studying the backs of baseball cards—.266 looked like a batting average.

I know now it to be something else as well.

It was my blood alcohol level on Christmas night, 2008—actually, the early hours of Dec. 26, to be accurate. That was the night I went to Parkland Hospital with a fractured skull, possibly spilling some of those batting averages and other sports-related numbers that have been spinning around in my brain for so many years along with, yes, an amount of blood the hospital report lists as "significant—can't stop."

Considering that the legal limit for operating a motor vehicle in the state of Texas is .08, some people might consider .08 to be a significant amount of alcohol. Honestly, I don't think it's that much even to this day. I think you set the law at .08 to try to keep people from driving when they're at .14 or .15. But .266—that's, shall we say, in another ballpark.

It's a figure I wasn't certain that I had reached until the summer of 2011 when I started working on this book. I remembered someone in the hospital talking to me shortly before I checked out on Dec. 29, saying that a .26 blood alcohol level was extremely dangerous and that I needed to curtail my drinking immediately.

I thought maybe it was a ploy. I don't even remember what the man looked like but he wasn't anyone who had consulted with me or spoke to me the previous three days. I'm not sure he was a doctor, seemed more like an administrative type. I thought maybe this was something that all the drunks were told as they were leaving the hospital, sort of Parkland's own "scared straight" tactic.

Not that I completely doubted its veracity. But it wasn't until a neurologist friend was able to find it in Parkland's records one summer afternoon in 2011, two years into my self-imposed sobriety, that I knew for sure that I had, in fact, been hauled out of an ambulance—just a few hours after celebrating a completely sober Christmas with my kids—with a .266.

The way I saw it: Slightly higher than Roger Maris' career average.

The way my neurologist explained it, honest to God: "That's a very respectable blood alcohol level."

Thanks, Doc. I tried.

This is not an anti-drinking book. I wouldn't care to read a book of that type and I surely wouldn't know how to write one. I was in love with alcohol for 35 years. It was a love affair that lasted longer than either of my marriages and certainly longer than any of my affairs. We had a good run, me and beer, from the early days when pounding down those cans of Budweiser made the hangovers worthwhile to that last great run with Stella Artois.

Oh, Stella. I first met her in New York City at P. J. Clarke's and at the bar that took over the new Runyon's spot on 2nd after the old Runyon's had closed around the corner. It seems like I drank it on visits to Washington, D.C. for Cowboys-Redskins games as well, but the Belgium brew wasn't distributed nationally at the time. When you look forward to Stella's arrival date in Dallas (February, 2005, select bars) as enthusiastically as I did, it might have been time to recognize that there was a problem.

But that would take four more years, a trip to one hospital with a fractured skull, time missed from work, a trip to another hospital following a seizure, and, oh yeah, did I mention some time behind bars—not in that order—before I would decide that this was an affair that really needed to cross the finish line.

I can't blame that on Stella. Put that one on her more dangerous half-sister, Stoli.

If I was in love with beer for most of my adult life, I became a serial stalker of vodka in my late 40s and early 50s. It didn't have to be Stoli, that's just what I usually ordered in bars because it was a buck cheaper than Grey Goose. But it could have been the Goose. Could have been Svedka (really reasonably priced and just as good as the premium brands, I highly recommend—oh, wait, that's going to have to be a different book) or even the tasteless Skyy. Hell, at home it was frequently the plastic 1.75 L bottle of Gordon's that did the trick which, basically, consisted of putting me to sleep at night.

But like I said, it was mostly a good run because I was mostly a good drunk. Funny most of the time. Even charming to some. Dare I say sexy? Why not? It's my book.

But not violent, not in the least. Much, much more likely to simply walk out of a party or a bar than to turn angry even in the slightest sense.

That's probably why it lasted as long as it did. If I had been waking up on a regular basis in jail or with cuts and bruises covering my body from a lost fight, I might have figured out that drinking—for me—was a lost cause much sooner.

This is not a self-help book. I am by no means a regular reader of self-help books, so why would I attempt to write one?

Now I don't doubt that there are people who can derive some benefit from hearing what a life fueled by alcohol, initially, did for me. In fact, I saw drinking as something that helped me in my work on many occasions. I know this to be a fact—before the bastard turned on me and sent me to jail and nearly killed me on Christmas night, 2008, and, yes, played a role in a marriage gone off the rails.

I know there are people who can benefit simply from the reaction I received from writing one column in the *Dallas*

Morning News in the summer of 2009 after the news of the Texas Rangers' Josh Hamilton's relapse became public knowledge. It was overwhelming.

Normally, anything I write about the Cowboys is going to get 3-4 times the response of anything I write about the Rangers. But this was huge, the emails, the text messages and the personal comments dwarfing the usual reaction to anything about the Cowboys and Rangers put together. Because this was about something else.

I was not even three months into my self-imposed sobriety at the time, so I was fully aware that I was barely out of the starting blocks. I had been reluctant to mention it publicly for that reason, but in this case with Hamilton's story having taken another turn, I thought the timing was right.

The point then and the point now is that you don't have to be an All-Star center fielder with a past history of alcohol and drug abuse. You don't have to be the completely-out-of-your-mind star of *Two and a Half Men*. You don't have to have a history of crime or violence, you don't have to produce a resume of life in and out of rehab facilities to recognize that what once was perhaps a reasonable level of social drinking meant to help you fit into your circle of co-workers, sorority sisters, high school buddies, etc. can reach an entirely different and more damaging level.

The fact that you can point to a friend and say, "He's way worse than me," doesn't necessarily mean you should feel good about taking yourself off the hook. The fact that you aren't the drunkest guy at the party or you aren't the girl who always seems to have the easiest access to drugs doesn't mean you don't need to pull back on the reins just a bit.

And, if my last few years have indicated anything, if you are scared of the idea of rehab clinics and don't really gravitate towards the camaraderie of AA meetings, maybe this can be for you, too. I never went to rehab and my only trip to an AA meeting in 2010 was to support a friend.

Don't get me wrong. I would be more out of my mind now than I was on Christmas night, 2008, to say I'm against rehab clinics or Alcoholics Anonymous. Without a doubt, rehab facilities have turned around thousands of lives. I know for a fact that AA has added years—good, quality years—to my father's life.

I'm saying only that what works for one person might not necessarily benefit the next one. My decision to stop drinking didn't have anything to do with a team of medical professionals working to get me sober. It wasn't about 12 steps, a support group or a belief in God.

Before I had become a drunk commenting on sports in the *Dallas Morning News* and on ESPN, I had been drunk on sports at a very early age. I needed to find a path back to those days.

Back to when .266 was nothing more to ponder than the batting average on a lazy, summer day.

That's where this journey began. In Tulsa, Oklahoma. With one really bad baseball card trade.

Based on other personal decisions I would make in life, not to mention more than a few failed prediction columns over four decades, some might have called that trade a sign of things to come.

CHAPTER 1

OKIES

"Memories can be distorted. They're just an interpretation, not a record. And they're irrelevant if you have the facts."

—Leonard Shelby (Guy Pearce) in *Memento*

MY MEMORY IS not as fucked up as you might think it would be after 35 years of drinking. It has its gaps to be sure. Mostly that's the hours of 1 to 3 a.m. on any given night from about 2002 to 2009. Let's say give or take a year on the front end of that, OK? For me, that's the closing time on the part of the brain that stores memories called the hippocampus, which sounds like something you might find in the Big Ten, but I didn't say that.

Anyway, in the film cited above, Shelby had anterograde amnesia. He couldn't form new memories.

That's a rare problem and it's not mine. I'm just one of the millions out there who have destroyed a number of brain cells through countless hours spent with drink in hand at pubs and lobby bars and, yes, by myself on my own cushy sofa.

But, more recently, I earned extra credit on the brain damage front, and that's why I've spent some time in the last year or two gathering facts about my behavior, about acts I do not remember.

Found some. Still searching for a few of the more important ones, like:

...Where exactly did I think I was going on the night of July 20, 2007 that I wound up in Caddo Mills instead of Coppell? For those not entirely familiar with the geography of the Dallas-Fort Worth area, those two towns are separated by about 34 miles. You have to go north and west from downtown Dallas to get to Coppell. You travel south, then east and cross a long bridge over Lake Ray Hubbard to reach Caddo Mills.

Driving alone, I thought I was headed home to one city.

Instead, I wound up handcuffed on the side of the road in the other.

...After spending a great afternoon with my kids, my brother, his kids and our parents on Christmas Day, 2008— consuming no alcohol during this time, mind you—how long could I have even been at a McKinney Ave. bar watching Blazers-Mavericks with friends before I found myself riding in an ambulance to Parkland Hospital with an open head wound?

And how did I achieve a blood alcohol level of .26 so fast?

...On May 7, 2009, during a commercial break of a local radio show with my good friends Ben Rogers and Skin Wade, how did I end up on the floor, suffering from a seizure? Was it triggered by the damage I had done in fracturing my skull the previous Christmas as predicted by my doctor?

Even now I can only provide answers to some of the above. I have obtained only a few facts as they relate to these incidents. I have some scattered memories of these moments that, better late than never, brought a conclusion to my 35-year drinking career.

As any alcoholic can tell you, it's a conclusion that could become a temporary one at any time. With one raised index finger towards a bartender, one single request for a Stoli-soda-splash of cranberry, it could be put on hold.

Let's be honest about this whole "no more drinks" thing. We could be talking about nothing more than a stay of execution here.

Like most people who drink far more than they should, this is not the first time I've stopped drinking. It's merely the first time I have attempted to quit.

The only difference between those two is—well, everything.

I stopped for 100 days once in the late 1990s when I was still covering the Dallas Stars as a beat writer for the *Dallas Morning News*. My regular drinking partner on the road, the Stars' travel director, quit with me.

We tried going to movies instead of pounding pints. In LA one Saturday night, we saw *As Good As It Gets.*

As a lifestyle, this wasn't. So when the 100 days were up, I went to Vegas.

Later, after being promoted to lead sports columnist, I quit for the entire 2000 NFL season.

(Not the pre-season, naturally. Be serious. Everybody needs a couple of stiff drinks to make their way through the pre-season).

In Tampa prior to the Baltimore Ravens-New York Giants Super Bowl that concluded that season, I wrote an advance column inspired by Edgar Allan Poe's *The Raven*.

I offer you the column here in its entirety. It ran in the *Sunday Morning News* in the days when spending money was the only way to get newspaper content (what a concept!), and yet here you here are getting it free of charge. Or possibly free on top of what you paid for the book, I suppose. Still, your lucky day.

* * *

With all due respect to my old friend, Ed Poe, for whom the Ravens were named:

*

Once upon a Super Sunday, dreaming of an idle Monday,
Pondering many a quaint and curious quote sheet filled with future lore,
Just before I fell to napping, suddenly there came a tapping,
As of someone gently rapping, rapping at my 22nd floor door.
"'Tis some beat writer," I muttered,
"And how'd he get on the concierge floor?"
"Housekeeping," said the voice. And nothing more.

*

This intrusion I recall now, for it forced my
thoughts to halt, how
So many fine defenders would descend on
offenses poor,
And the poorest was the Ravens' whose
attack was all but cravin'
For the presence of a passer, a passer to
become the toast of Baltimore.
"Can it be this man named Dilfer is equipped
to slam the door?"
Doubt the Ravens? Nevermore.

*

For it seems this team of transplants, former
Browns and one-time miscreants,
Is the team destined to win the Super Bowl
after XXXIV,
Scoring points may be the rage now but Kurt
Warner's left the stage now,
And the NFC's owned by Giants, far from
meek at 14-4.
Run and pass they hope to balance but
through the wall of Baltimore?
Bet the Giants? Whatever for?

*

There was little notice taken when this new
club called the Ravens
Took to building up a defense like one never
seen before,
Men like Lewis and McCrary did not falter,
did not tarry
As the backs they coldly buried could not
help their teams to score.

By year's end, there was one number to
show what Ravens had encumbered,
How their enemies had slumbered.
Shutouts—four by Baltimore.

*

So I sense the Jints are dreaming when they
say that they are scheming
Ways and means to put a beating on the
heads of Baltimore.
For it's not the arm of Dilfer and the balls the
Giants pilfer
Or even Sehorn's looks to kill for that will
help the Giants score.
It's the ghost of John Unitas that will carry
Baltimore. (In overtime once more).
Doubt the Ravens? Nevermore.

      —Copyright 2001 *The Dallas Morning News*

I bring you this column (or almost half of it, actually), not simply because I correctly picked the Ravens to win. I wrote this column in the final week of a five-month period in which I consumed nothing more dangerous than a non-alcoholic beer. I wrote it when I had time to write it. It took about 20 hours total and required staying in my room a couple of nights when Super Bowl party passes were calling me.

This is not to brag about how much effort I put into writing a column. I am trying to convey the opposite here. I exhausted about 19 more hours than I normally require to write a column because suddenly, with no beers to be consumed and no vodka to chase it with, I had a lot of god damn time on my hands at a Super Bowl, of all places.

Don't get me wrong, I'm not here to tell you that this is the greatest sports column ever penned or even one of the finer efforts at sports-page poetry (although you gotta know Jay-Z wishes he had been the first to rhyme "Dilfer, Giants pilfer and Sehorn looks to kill for").

I'm just saying that it would have been nice had it occurred to me back then that with a little less drinking (or maybe a lot less), some extra time for writing would have appeared out of nowhere on a regular basis.

But, shit. That didn't happen. When I got home from the Super Bowl, I had proved to myself—no one else was remotely interested—that I could go an entire season without a drink. That could only mean that I did not have a drinking problem.

That's the kind of accomplishment that called for a few shots, don't you think?

I did.

Long before I knew what it was to be drunk, even before my father gave his 8-year-old son a sip of Rheingold beer (pretty nasty stuff to a regular drinker, just imagine what a warm Rheingold tastes like to a second-grader on the beach at Montauk Point), I was drunk on sports.

My older brother, Pat, sparked my interest in sports. He was the better athlete, and by athlete, I'm using that word as it applies to your average suburban white kids of the 60s. Let's put it this way.

As a senior at Richardson High School just outside of Dallas, he quit the basketball team because he was too busy studying his way to becoming salutatorian in a graduating class of over 900 to put up with coming off the bench.

That same coach, Jerry Stone, who would later achieve the minor degree of fame that he deserved as Spud Webb's junior college coach, cut me as a sophomore. I remain convinced my release was more latent hostility that Stone had built up towards my brother than any misgivings he had about my total disregard for anything that resembled bending over or moving my feet to play defense.

I was momentarily devastated but angry mostly that my two best friends had not yet been cut. When they came walking into study hall a week later, sheepish grins barely hiding the pain of their basketball careers also lying in ruins, I was OK with it.

After a junior high career that produced just one point (on a technical foul), I had pretty much given up on the idea of becoming a 5-foot-11 version of John Havlicek, anyway.

But long before my basketball career and my brother's unraveled separately in the RHS Gym, we cultivated our love for the game together in the basement of our New Providence, N.J. home. We played 1-on-1 full court which, I believe, measured about 35 feet.

I was in first and second-grade, Pat in fifth and sixth. Certain concessions were made on my behalf. He was not allowed to block my shots which seemed fair since I sure as hell wasn't about to leap up and block any of his. The baskets, attached directly to concrete basement walls with no backboards were roughly seven feet high.

When we weren't down in the basement playing sports, we were in the den watching them.

Now if you want to develop a serious interest in sports, try becoming aware of the game of baseball when the team that's on TV every day is the '61 Yankees.

But I have gotten ahead of the story here, jumping all the way to age six.

(I told you that my memory wasn't that fucked up). Before arriving in New Jersey in March of '61, the Cowlishaws were just a bunch of happy Okies. I was the big city kid, having been born in Tulsa on March 31, 1955. My brother was born in Muskogee, my mom in Bartlesville and my dad— well, you don't even want to go there. It was called Wolco and hasn't been on a map since maybe the Eisenhower administration. If you are determined to place his roots, put him in Skiatook, where he actually drove the school bus as a high school junior before heading off to the Pacific in WW II.

(I'm thinking school districts were a little less anxious over liability in those days, my dad driving the muddy farm roads to pick up his friends en route to school each morning).

I had been only vaguely aware of sports being televised when we lived in Tulsa. I was five, give me a break.

At that point, sports meant only two things to me— baseball cards and electric football.

I'm not sure if the one and only baseball card trade of my kindergarten year was a sign of horrible fantasy deals I would make later in life, a precursor of awful investments I would seek or a combination of both.

Somehow I traded a 1960 Mickey Mantle card for a 1960 New York Yankees team card, convinced by a ruthless neighbor that we shall call Jimmy Blackburn (because we think it was him) that I was getting "all" the Yankees while he was settling for one in return.

Now none of us knew that Mantle cards would one day be worth hundreds, some of them even thousands of dollars. Otherwise, I would not have made a regular habit (brace yourself, card lovers, this is going to hurt) of thumb-tacking my favorite cards to a bulletin board or writing in ink on the backs of the cards to update statistics.

Ouch.

Whatever is the opposite of 'Mint Condition,' that's what became of most of my cards. That was the case with the great players, anyway.

Still, on the day of that fateful trade, I quickly learned both the value of superstar cards and of having a big brother who could visit the neighbor's house and, um, rescind ill-conceived trades I had been suckered into. Nine-year-old Pat made a quick visit to the Blackburn house. I got my Mickey Mantle card back (one of the few I still have).

I'm sure that football cards had made their way into Tulsa five-and-dimes by 1960. But I don't recall having any in my possession until the move to New Jersey. Besides, football was about something else entirely.

Somewhere up our block there was an older boy named Wayne Lehman. When he wasn't painting model airplanes or cars, he was painting electric football players in glorious detail.

My San Francisco 49ers were gorgeous with their red jerseys and silver helmets. The silver numbers of the offensive starters were painted on front and back, so I could easily identify quarterback Y.A. Tittle.

(I'm not entirely certain what purpose it served to know which of your men was quarterback. If you think the New York Jets make the passing game appear difficult in today's world, you should have seen an electric football player attempting to launch a tiny ball of cotton with any accuracy 50 years ago).

My brother's team was the Philadelphia Eagles. I suppose that meant he got to celebrate their championship win over Green Bay that season. All I know is it meant he had Ted Dean in his backfield.

Dean's face was painted brown. The NFL was mostly a white man's game in 1960, but Good ol' Wayne was a stickler for accuracy. If there were Negroes on NFL offenses, then by God there would be Negroes in electric football in this all-white neighborhood of Tulsa, OK.

That, along with a few faces on baseball cards my brother allowed in my care after the dubious Mantle trade, was my limited introduction to race.

(This sounds crazy, I know, but I have memories of my 49ers not being able to catch Dean in the open field).

The NFL was a long way from America's game at that stage. Once we made the move to New Jersey in 1961, I can recall watching an NFL highlights show on Saturday nights featuring an announcer (identified through the magic of the Internet as Jim Leaming) who would open each show, saying, "There's action a-plenty, so let's get with it."

Mind you, this action consisted of watching highlights from the previous Sunday's games six days later.

Even if Tittle, somehow seeming to move with me to the New York metropolitan area, was elevating the Giants to the top of the NFC East, their games weren't televised in New Jersey on Sunday afternoons.

While the NFL was carefully limiting its TV audience, the Yankees were not. Day or night, home or road, the Yankees dominated our living room. My brother, displaying skills he would only refine years later at Stanford Law School, claimed the Yankees as his sole property.

Whether on TV or in the backyard whiffle ball games, I settled for the Detroit Tigers. And by settling, I mean I had a team with Norm Cash hitting .361, Rocky Colavito driving in 140 runs, Yankee-killer Frank Lary collecting 23 of the Tigers' 101 wins in 1961.

And they lost to the Yankees by eight games.

Even if I was not inclined to root for the Yankees, I was lucky enough to see one of Maris' record-breaking 61 home runs in person.

OK, it was only No. 7 in an early season Sunday game against the Baltimore Orioles. And I am told I slept through the last five innings.

That's why I'm going to skip the part where, as a dutiful baseball writer, I spend three or four obligatory paragraphs telling you how I remember coming out of the subway and into this giant Stadium, its steel edifice reaching towards the sky, and then I looked down and saw the greenest grass in the world, a thing I had never imagined while watching games at home on our black-and-white Motorola.

Instead, I'll be honest. Yes, it was fun to go to Yankee Stadium that first time and the two or three other visits that we made before moving to Texas in the summer of 1963. Yes, we had only a black-and-white TV at home.

But you know what? Walking into the stadium, I was a pretty bright kid and I already knew there was going to be a shitload of green grass out there, so I wasn't entirely moved by the experience.

Although our stay in New Jersey was a mere two years-plus, it is a shame (in this one case, anyway) that we were not yet part of the completely crazed picture-snapping society we inhabit today.

We went to Yankee Stadium, we visited the Polo Grounds to see the Mets in the summer of '63, we saw a Rangers-Maple Leafs game at the old Madison Square Garden on 49th street and saw the Harlem Globetrotters play there, too, as part of a doubleheader with a Knicks game.

There are no pictures, programs, ticket stubs to record these events.

It would be fun to see pictures from those formative years. It might spark something in the memory banks that are basically limited to knowledge of a Maris homer and a memory of Mantle hitting one out on a rainy day against Cleveland. Oh, and this I recall, too. The hockey game was delayed quite a while after a goalie took a puck in the face.

Seriously, why the fuck didn't that happen all the time back then? Could no one launch a puck with those weak-ass uncurved Northland sticks in 1962?

But when I think about how I got started down this sports-writing, sports-talking path, there's no question that those early trips to some of the greatest sports landmarks in our nation played a pivotal role.

It's not like I had an Al Pacino as Frank Serpico moment where I saw a gathering of cops investigating a crime and said, "I wanna know what they know." I didn't look at the press box at Yankee Stadium or Madison Square Garden and think any such thing. I doubt I knew that a press box existed.

But it was that fascination with sports that drove me to the newspapers for late scores, for the updated standings, for the TV guide that would tell me when I could watch the next week's games. My parents—God bless 'em—always subscribed to at least two newspapers both in New Jersey and then in the Dallas suburbs where we moved in the summer of '63.

I was too young to read and appreciate the great New York sportswriters of that time. By junior high in Dallas, though, I sure as hell knew the difference between Blackie Sherrod and anyone else at the *Times Herald* or the *Morning News*.

And I determined long before getting the ax from the 10th grade basketball team that my future in sports was not as a player or a coach but as a reporter, a writer, maybe if I got really, really lucky even as a columnist.

The notion of battling Woody Paige in showdowns wouldn't enter my beer-soaked brain—or somebody else's troubled mind—for some time.

CHAPTER 2

THE LIQUOR CABINET

"I know, I know, many questions.
But first, (drink) the tranya."

—*Star Trek*, "The Corbomite Maneuver"

TO THE REST of America, 1969 was the Summer of
Love or the Summer of Woodstock or the summer that the
Cubs almost got the job done but ultimately failed because
the Mets' pitching went crazy and the Cubs did what they always do.

It was all of those things to me, too, I guess although the
Woodstock part would not register until I was sitting uncom-
fortably next to my parents in the gone-but-not-forgotten
Preston Royal theatre in north Dallas.

Uncomfortable because you just didn't see a lot of nudity
in the big screen in 1970. Hell, you don't see that much of it
now, either, and if you do, at least someone on the screen is
likely to be marginally attractive.

But for me 1969 was something very different. It was the summer that we buried my mother, Wanda. Dead of breast cancer at 42.

I'm not sure I spent enough time reflecting on her death at the time. I don't think I've ever truly reflected on what it has meant to me even four decades later.

But in 1969, I was 14. She had been quietly battling cancer for six years without complaint. We had learned to make do without her at certain times for certain things.

But your mom being unavailable for dinner or for attending the occasional Cowboys game in the Cotton Bowl is different from your mom just one day being gone. For good.

My brother, four years older, left for Stanford in the fall of '69. A house that had been a happy home for four was suddenly half full.

My father, successfully working his ranks through the Zale Corporation at the time—the founder, Morris B. Zale, would refer to him as the company's "highest ranking Gentile"—was a busy, busy man. He put in long hours five days a week, almost always at least half-days of work on Saturdays and there were frequent road trips to jewelry stores across the country.

I didn't quite live by myself and almost never spent the night alone, usually staying with friends or at my cousin's house in Plano.

But when you're 14 and you feel like you've been a little screwed over in having lost your mom at a young age, you think whatever side benefits you can discover are rightfully yours.

I was a good kid. I did not go wild. But having been left to fend myself now and then, I merely got creative.

If I wanted to see one of the Mets games in the World Series—they had become my Mets since you recall my brother had the Yankees locked down—there were no DVRs to rely upon. The World Series was still two years away from its first night game.

I can't tell you why I skipped school and stayed home to watch Game 4 instead of Game 5 which proved to be the clincher. Maybe I had a test the next day. Maybe we had a basketball game the day of Game 5 (not that my skills were needed during the game—only my ability to produce a shot chart on a clipboard afterwards).

Regardless, I skipped school the day that Tom Seaver helped the Mets to a commanding 3-1 lead over the heavily favored Orioles. Maybe I skipped a couple of other days here and there, using my early writing skills to forge my father's signature on notes a day later.

If it was all in the sake of researching events for a lifetime to be spent chronicling the sports world, surely that was justified.

Leading a more solitary existence than most ninthgraders also gave me access to my father's liquor cabinet. Again, I didn't go wild with it. That would come later in life.

My father was primarily a scotch drinker and not much of one at that. The bourbon was there mostly for show, I guess, or perhaps for some potential dinner party that never quite materialized.

Thus, as long as I slowly reduced the quantity of Jim Beam available, there was minimal chance of discovery. Mix that with the long hours my father was working to go with the misery and loneliness that must have invaded his life without Wanda, his wife of 22 years, and I was home free.

But really I think tracing the roots of my love affair with alcohol to the occasional bourbon-and-coke in 9th grade is going back just a bit too far. I never got anywhere close to drunk on the stuff and frankly didn't really care for the taste. It just seemed like part of the process of growing up in addition to being something I could do that separated me from a more focused and accomplished older brother.

I tend to think a more accurate (and, by chance, sporting!) beginning to my drinking days came two years later.

In 1971, the drinking age in Texas was 21. It would soon become 18 but that was a couple of years away. I can't speak for other Dallas area high schools, but around the hallowed halls of Richardson High, it was well known that a convenience store called Pedigo's down in the Oak Lawn area was willing to provide beer to younger consumers.

No fake IDs necessary. Just bring cash.

I was 16 in the fall of '71 but I looked 14. At best. If I was shaving, it was with an electric razor and strictly for practice.

By this time, I had sipped a Budweiser or two. But never more than that. With a weekend trip to Lake Tawakoni with friends looming, it was time to grow up. Or at least this was what I thought growing up entailed.

Although *American Graffiti* would not come out for a couple more years, I must have been channeling Toad as he attempts to buy liquor without an ID ("Yeah, uhh, let me have a Three Musketeers, uhh, a ball point pen there, a comb, pint of Old Harper, couple of flashlight batteries and some of that beef jerky…") because, on a Friday night before leaving for the lake, I nervously lined up several objects for purchase along with a six-pack of—could it be?

Yes. Ballantine beer.

There were two primary beverages that served as sponsors on Yankee games in the early '60s. One was a truly awful chocolate product called Yoo-Hoo. The only thing it had going for it was the cartoon figure of Yogi Berra making a sensational catch in left field.

(Announcer: "Look at Yogi. He's running straight up the wall!"

Yogi: "Me-hee for Yoo-hoo, too-hoo.")

The other was the beer sponsor. The Mets had Rheingold. The Yankees, I figured at the time, had chosen the classier beer.

("Baseball and Ballantine, baseball and Ballantine… What a combination… All across the nation! Baseball and… Ball-an-tine!")

It would be several hours, not much food and five cans of Ballantine, the last two a bit on the too-warm side, before I was leaning out the driver's window of my '66 Cutlass convertible parked somewhere along the shores of Lake Tawakoni to puke my guts out.

While learning the next morning exactly what a hangover involves, I could have gone a few different directions. Could have vowed to never drink again (but doesn't everyone do that during that first miserable "day after"?). Could have vowed to monitor my drinking a little more closely.

Instead, I decided that Ballantine was one horseshit beer—an opinion seconded by a friend I had talked into getting his own six—and I was going back to Budweiser—if and when this monstrous headache ever went away.

* * *

Growing up, I was never as focused as my brother when it came to—well, just about everything. He graduated second in a class of more than 900 in 1969. I graduated somewhere in the 200-300 range of a slightly smaller group at Richardson High School in 1973.

In fifth grade, Pat wrote on a class paper, "I plan to grow up to be a lawyer."

By God if he didn't.

By the time I was in high school, I thought enough about being a sportswriter that I took journalism classes and wrote sports stories for the *Talon*, the school paper. To all the e-mailers who think I suck as a columnist today, if only you could have seen me then...

But you can't, and I'm not going to help you. If any clippings remain in an attic somewhere, I'm sure as shit not hunting for them just to prove I had a mountain of clichés to fight through just to get to mediocre.

I grew up assuming I would go to the University of Texas in Austin for two reasons. One, I was a huge fan of the football team. If you think that hype and trash-talking had not been invented in 1969, clearly you weren't a ninth-grader dealing with rabid Arkansas fans (really, what the hell were they thinking?) on a daily basis for months leading up to The

Shootout. That's the game where Texas escaped Fayetteville with a 15-14 win as President Nixon congratulated Darrell Royal, who looked to be in a state of disbelief after his team's fourth quarter comeback.

By the way, even Nixon said he would have been a sportswriter if he hadn't had gone the politician route. If you think that might have made for a better country, hey, that's a different book. And it's been done.

The second reason I figured I would be a Longhorn was that it was one school I knew I could get into.

Yes. Times have changed drastically on that front.

But Sara Scott, my high school journalism teacher, had talked up Missouri and its long history of producing successful reporters. When I got the letter saying that I had been accepted, I figured I was bound for Columbia, even though I had never been there.

(Turns out I was off by 36 years as my daughter Rachel would become the first Cowlishaw to take any journalism classes there in the fall of 2009. M-I-Z...!)

But a few days later, a surprising acceptance letter arrived from the University of Colorado. I say surprising because after being rejected by North Carolina, I figured Missouri to be the only out-of-state school likely to offer its services.

Now I had what I might have called a conundrum, although guessing from my 530 Verbal SAT score, I might not have.

Missouri offered a future in journalism.

Colorado offered 3.2 beer.

That sounds like something I might fabricate, a scenario that fits a little too snugly into a book about someone whose rise in the media world would cross paths with, maybe even occasionally benefit from, his love for malt-based beverages.

It also happens to be true.

And so with *Baba O'Riley* blaring from the 8-track speakers of my '71 Montego, I set off for Boulder.

I mean, Colorado had to have a student paper, too, right?

* * *

My time as a Buff was a good time, but it lasted only a year. I drank as much 3.2 beer as the next freshman, nothing outrageous. I made friends with a number of CU's football players, many of whom lived in the dorm.

At the Saints-Colts Super Bowl, I reminded Colts defensive backs coach Rod Perry of a winning touchdown pass he threw me the one day in spring after we talked a number of the players into joining us for a game of two-hand touch.

Shockingly, that pass proved more memorable to me than it did to Perry.

The next year I like to think of as my redshirt year. I worked at a sporting goods store in Dallas' trendy new (at the time) NorthPark mall and took nine hours of night school classes at Richland Junior College.

We liked to call it searching for ourselves back then. In the meantime—yes, this was a different era—I met two Cowboys' players who took summer jobs as salesmen at the sporting goods store.

Defensive end Harvey Martin sold shoes in the back. Other than to meet him, I did not get to know him well. But customers came in and laughed and loved it as the 6-foot-5 Martin lowered his frame to straddle the stool and sell them running shoes.

Wide receiver Drew Pearson worked in the athletics department in the center of the store with me. Mostly, he stood around and told stories. He was gracious, humble and not overly interested in selling merchandise. I even got him to help me take the trash out back to the dumpster one day.

Harvey and Drew were making $3.20 an hour. This is the God's honest truth. I remember that because the rest of us were making $2.25 and kind of pissed off about their starting salaries.

Over the years, Drew and I have had lots of laughs about those days. And if I have written more than once that he deserved a spot in the Cowboys' Ring of Honor—finally gaining that reward in the fall of 2011—it's because he did, dammit, not because we used to sell jocks and socks alongside each other in the summer of '75.

* * *

When I finally arrived on the UT campus in the fall of '75, it was as a Radio-TV-Film major, not a journalist.

I had taken an "Introduction to Film" class at Richland in the spring taught by the late, great Allan Calkin. Although I was certainly a movie buff at an earlier age, Big Al taught me an entirely new way to look at film. We talked for hours about movies and had many cocktails at the old Knox Street Pub, the one that was actually on Knox Street.

Al was also the first gay man I ever slept with and...

(READERS: Timeout! Whoa, Tim, hold on there. That sort of came from out of left field. We expected to read a few confessions about your drinking and maybe some really inappropriate misadventures behind the wheel of a car while drunk, but just exactly where are you going with this thing?)

...and the reason that happened is because one night while watching movies at his apartment he knew I'd had too much to drink, too much Rum-and-Gatorade if you must know, to drive back to my apartment on Park Lane, so he insisted I stay.

On his couch. I wasn't his type.

Seriously, Al was a great friend for years. He was in the closet then, but came out later and became an activist in the Democratic Party before contracting AIDS and dying of liver failure in 1989.

Al pushed me to stop selling ping pong tables and gym shorts at NorthPark and get down to UT to study film, critique film, and do something in the film industry. And that truly was my intention right up until the moment that I realized students had to spend all night in the halls of the Communication Center to sign up for a basic RTF class as an indication of their dedication and desire.

An all-nighter or two outside the Erwin Center in order to secure sixth-row tickets to Springsteen in 1979? Not a problem. I could handle that.

An all-nighter to study for a test or to simply sign up for a class?

Motivation wasn't one of my strengths in the '70s.

But in the summer of '76 as I stayed in Austin to attend summer school and begin making up a few of those hours lost during my redshirt campaign, I saw an ad in the *Daily Texan* seeking staff writers for the summer.

Pretty much just like that, I was back in journalism.

* * *

Two moments stand out from my last two years at UT that would serve as signals for what was to come later in life.

One was that as a senior in the fall of 1977, I was allowed to write columns.

And so the opening paragraph of the first column I authored for the *Daily Texan* began: "One game into Earl Campbell's senior season, his Heisman Trophy hopes are all but gone."

OK, let me explain something to those who would suggest I have followed this inauspicious start with 30 more years of God-awful predictions.

One is that the Longhorns had gone 5-5-1, a fifth-place team in an eight-team Southwest Conference, the previous year. The relatively unknown Fred Akers had not only replaced Darrell Royal but scrapped our hallowed Wishbone offense in the process.

Two, Campbell had averaged fewer than 1,000 yards rushing his first three seasons as a Longhorn. It was only under Akers that Campbell was forced to lose 25 pounds, to display speed to go with all that power. And it was hardly evident in that season-opening win over Boston College as to exactly what Earl was about to become.

So there. It was a prediction with a strong foundation. It just happened to be wildly wrong.

A month later, my Yankees were in the World Series.

Yes, my Yankees. Somehow during all the lean years of Bobby Murcer, Roy White, Horace Clarke and that still troubling family swap between Fritz Petersen and Mike Kekich, I had been allowed to adopt what was no longer a championship franchise from my brother who was otherwise occupied in Stanford Law School.

With my roommate Mike Donovan having spent formative years in Upper Montclair, N.J., we watched the Yankees win Game 1 over the Dodgers while consuming many beers. It seemed important to us to see just what sort of headline was being prepared for the Yankees' first win of a World Series game in 13 years (they had been swept by the Big Red Machine in '76), so we drove to the *Daily Texan* to find out.

Smoking victory cigars, our behavior was considered a bit too obnoxious by the earnest student journalists in the *Texan* office, so we decided to take our celebration to a bar. As I was driving down The Drag (Guadalupe St.), my roommate instructed me to stop so he could grab a newspaper and see what bands might be performing nearby.

While he stood outside the car flipping through the paper, I took off.

It might have been customary to my friends later in life to see me just wander off from a bar, a party, wherever when I determined I had had enough to drink. It was not something Mike expected since we lived about five miles away on Lamar.

I decided to drive to our favorite dive bar, the Posse, but somewhere along the way I clipped a curb. By clipped, I mean I destroyed both the right-side tires on my yellow

Malibu Classic and drove the last three or four miles home on the rims.

Waking up to look for my car in the morning is something I probably did 15 or 20 times in my life. Waking up to inspect the damage is something I did three times in my life.

For some, that sort of embarrassment along with the realization of the more serious damage that one might have inflicted can be a life-changing event.

For me, other than the time that I forced an angry college roommate to call another friend to get a ride home, it was something I became pretty damn good at hiding from the world.

CHAPTER 3

THE '80S

"You got paid on Friday, your pockets are jinglin'
And you see the lights, you get all tinglin'
'cause you're cruisin' with a six
Lookin' for the heart of Saturday night."

—Tom Waits, *Heart of Saturday Night*

THE '80S WERE a good decade to be a drinking man. Or so it seemed at the time.

In what looks like something of a whirlwind, gazing back at it now, I lived in Corpus Christi, Oklahoma City, Dallas, San Francisco and Dallas again. I lived in five apartments, bought a house, sold the house, lived in two more apartments, bought a house and then rented that house while living in a rental 1500 miles away.

A time of change?

There were two marriages and one divorce. I worked for four newspapers, one of them twice. In that span I covered high school football, basketball and baseball in Corpus Christi, high school football, minor league baseball and college basketball in Oklahoma City, the SMU Mustangs, Southwest Conference basketball, major league baseball and finally the Cowboys in Dallas, the Giants in San Francisco and then the Cowboys once more.

All that and only one arrest. Not bad.

It could have been a sign of a drinking problem that I began dating my college roommate's younger sister when I was a senior at UT and she was a freshman. We then married in 1982 after she finished college. We were essentially drinking pals. As someone with five brothers in an Irish Catholic family, four of them older than her, Marcie was famous—at least in our circles—for being someone who could hold her liquor.

That may have been the best connection we had. Two years into the marriage, I sensed trouble when she told me she was moving to Los Angeles with her boss. I'm intuitive that way. These sorts of things tend to put a damper on a relationship.

She asked if she could take the RX-7. I handed her the keys to the Honda Civic. End of first marriage.

There were no kids involved. The only real issue was a house we had just bought in Grand Prairie after I got to the *Morning News* in 1984, but beyond that one monetary complication, it was basically a marital mulligan.

She moved, and I moved on

Once I got out from under that house, I rented an apartment in Addison (north Dallas) near a small airport used primarily for private planes. I mention that because one night after a long evening of drinking down on Knox Ave., I made a wrong turn near the apartment and got lost driving amidst what appeared to be warehouses but are actually airplane hangars.

After a confusing few minutes trying to find my way off the property, I saw flashing lights in my rearview mirror.

An officer asked if knew where I was. My answer of "Love Field?" was deemed unacceptable.

My first experience with handcuffs followed.

Technically, I was not charged with a DWI because I was on private property and no one had issued a complaint. This was 1985. Drinking and driving was still an unsanctioned sport in the state of Texas. Eventually, I pled no contest to a charge of "illegal trespassing" and was placed on three months' probation. When that period ended, the arrest, the charge, and the plea were all erased from my record.

So, technically, if I say this never happened and I just made it up for the sake of this book, no one can prove otherwise. But it did happen, and it was nearly 25 years later—after I had begun my journey towards sobriety—before I told my parents about it.

I will be honest. It did not have a profound impact on my life. DWIs were not taken as seriously in 1985 as they are today. Not even close. Drinking and driving itself was not yet technically illegal in the state of Texas. There were no open container laws. If an officer pulled you over and you were drinking your first or second beer, he would tell you to throw them away and not to drink and drive.

Times have changed. For the better, yes.

It was this same time period—1984-85—that I covered baseball for the *Dallas Morning News*. Tim Kurkjian was the

Rangers' beat writer and I was the backup Rangers and major league writer. Kurkjian did not take a lot of time off but I made a few road trips with the team over those two seasons.

On one memorable night in Chicago, I counted as 18 Rangers—at one time or another—passed through the Lodge on Division St. The Lodge was known at the time for $1 Old Styles and a crowd that sang along with the jukebox at the top of their lungs until 4 a.m.

This is one of those things you ponder later in life when you stop drinking. *But what if I somehow find myself in the Lodge, it's 3 in the morning and Barry McGuire's "Eve of Destruction" comes on? You're telling me I can't have a beer while shouting, 'And even the Jordan River's got—bodies floatin'?*

It's not an exaggeration when I say I counted nearly three-fourths of the Rangers roster there that one night. Maybe a couple of coaches figured into the count. But this was, in my mind, nearing the end of those days where a base-ball beat writer would go out at night and see large gatherings of the players that he covered.

By the time I covered the Giants in 1988-89—and again made my regular pilgrimage to the Lodge for those Cubs games—the only player I ever saw there was pitcher Terry Mulholland. One of the nicer guys you could ever hope to cover, Mulholland even came over to me while playing the bowling shuffleboard game in the back of the bar and confessed, "Hey, Tim, I don't know a couple of these writers' names, help me out."

I hardly ever saw the Giants out on the town. Maybe Will Clark having a beer near the team hotel. I seem to recall buying Candy Maldonado a white Zinfandel or two at the

Hyatt bar in New York City where $7 beers in 1984 were considered obscene. I can only imagine what they charge today.

It's possible the Giants just didn't party as hard as the Rangers. That's probably going to be the case on a team with leaders like Dave Dravecky and Brett Butler as opposed to, say, Buddy Bell.

No offense, Buddy. You were much more fun.

But I think players already were moving away from being careless in the public eye, even before camera phones could record their every move. Those that went out found more private ways to go about it—clubs and the like—rather than to be seen in the same bars where sportswriters could afford to drink.

My most memorable drinking night while covering the Giants came in 1989 when the team was (again) in Chicago. The Warriors of T-M-C (Tim Hardaway, Mitch Richmond, Chris Mullin) had just upset Utah in the first round and were going to play Game 1 in Phoenix that night. Also, some guy named Jordan had just hit a fairly memorable shot to beat Cleveland in the first round, and so the Bulls were playing Game 1 in New York.

I went with several Giants writers to Harry Caray's near the hotel, and the bar portion of the restaurant was packed two, maybe three-deep along the bar. We were watching the Bulls-Knicks, but it was hard to get drinks. Meanwhile, the guy sitting directly in front of me had no problem getting served food, drinks, whatever he wanted. The female bartender seemed to think he was the only guy in the joint.

After stepping aside to get a closer look, I finally figured out it was John Cusack. I was already a big fan of *The Sure Thing* and *Sixteen Candles*, and *Say Anything* had just come out.

Well, we stayed even though there was no real hope of food for us. After Jordan had disposed of the Knicks in Game 1 and I had finished half a dozen beers, the crowd was thinning out before the Warriors game started. I approached Cusack at the bar and said I wanted to buy him and his friends a drink.

"No, let me buy you guys a round," he said.

And so for the next hour, Cusack—drinking Long Island Teas of all things—talked baseball with a bunch of Giants' writers, expressing fascination with how we got to travel the country watching them play.

Funny, we kind of thought he was the one with the great job.

At one point, I grabbed a potato chip from the bar and said to him, "Did you know these have 4 percent of the daily requirement of riboflavin," mimicking a line he uses to try to impress a girl in *The Sure Thing*.

Cusack's response: "Really?"

That's what I realized it's possible that actors memorize lines for a role and then dispatch them from their memory. Either that or Cusack was even drunker than I was…

By the end of that summer of '89, I had moved back to Dallas to cover the Cowboys. Not yet totally ready for kids, my wife and I decided to get a dog. I brought home an American Eskimo that Christmas.

Thus, Runyon entered our lives. By next summer, another American Eskimo named Lodge would follow. Dogs named Runyon and Lodge—have I mentioned a slight drinking problem?

* * *

For returning to the Cowboys' beat, drinking was not listed as a requirement, but for a team still rooted in a unique way of doing things that Tex Schramm had created, it should have been.

Jerry Jones and Jimmy Johnson were going to change the organization in extraordinary ways, but the importance Schramm had placed on alcohol would not be diminished.

The dining area directly behind press row at Texas Stadium became a full open bar once the game was over each Sunday. Writers covering the game, generally speaking, did not partake while crafting their work for the Monday papers. But once those stories were filed, there was no hurry to get to the parking lot and head home.

If alcohol in press boxes was fairly uncommon by the late '80s, what really set the Cowboys apart was life on the road.

I still remember in 1986, my first year on the beat, when longtime *Philadelphia Daily News* columnist Rich Hofmann was on the Eagles' beat. He was a good friend who would attend my wedding in 1987, and I was a groomsman in his wedding in '88 along with Fox's Ken Rosenthal (an Orioles beat writer at the time).

We were going to go to a bar in Philly to watch Game 1 of the Red Sox-Mets World Series. I told Hofmann to meet me at the Cowboys' hospitality suite and we'd have a drink there before going out.

Hofmann said, "The Cowboys' what?"

Yeah. The suite. The place where you run into the occasional assistant coach the night before the game. The place where the liquor flows. Tex wouldn't have had it any other way.

Neither would my rival on the beat, Jim Dent of the *Dallas Times Herald*. Dent has gone on to write several successful and critically acclaimed sports books in recent years. He was a troubled man in those days—not that he didn't break stories largely through Schramm that caused me something approaching ulcers—but I don't need to air anyone's dirty laundry but mine here. If you want to know why I wasn't the drunkest man in the room or the Cowboys' hospitality suite on a regular basis, you can Google Dent and see what I'm talking about.

Assistant coaches would stop by the hospitality suite a lot in those days. There was a time in 1987, the night before a pre-season game somewhere. I was talking to Jim Erkenbeck, the Cowboys' offensive line coach, an ex-Marine who had Lee Marvin's voice if not, come to think of it, his entire persona. Erkenbeck was making fun of me and my hopes of achieving my annual summer goal in Thousand Oaks—that was to run more miles than I drank beers during the five weeks spent there.

I'd always get off to a good start, stay in the first couple of nights and build up say a 12-1 lead for "miles over beers." By the second week the score was usually tied. By the third week I had come up with a different goal.

Erkenbeck laughed at me, then confided his own plan. "I'm just going to quit drinking when I turn 65," he said. Schramm, who had been on the fringe of the conversation, ever-present drink in his hand, injected his opinion.

"Don't be so damn sure about 65," he said.

CHAPTER 4

KNOCK, KNOCK,
KNOCKIN' ON JIMMY'S DOOR

"I'm on your side, nowhere to hide
Trapdoors that open, I spiral down…"

—*In Limbo*, Radiohead

IT IS A sunny spring day in 1992 at Valley Ranch, practice home of the Dallas Cowboys. Jimmy Johnson is not yet a Super Bowl-winning coach, just a guy who has turned the corner quickly by reaching the playoffs two years after that awful 1-15 start in 1989. He's enjoying having fun with the media again as he had in Miami. The sparring is on the playful side now. A playoff win over Chicago and a roster brimming with young Hall of Fame-bound talent equips Jimmy to jab back at reporters and columnists who had had so much fun at his and Jerry Jones' expense back in '89.

"Oh, there's just one thing I want to mention," Johnson says after answering the usual mundane questions that only an NFL mini-camp can inspire. "I'm around here all day and I make myself available to the media while I'm here. When I'm gone at the end of the day, my time is my time. One thing you never want to do is try to call me on the phone at home.

"But the WORST thing that one of you can ever do is come over to my house and knock on the door. I just want you to know that."

Johnson turns and walks down the track, heading towards his office. The reporters and TV photographers still gathered in a semi-circle look around with similarly puzzled expressions, silently asking each other, "Uhh—what the hell was that?"

Oh. Except me. I know exactly what Jimmy is saying, but not because I'm smarter or a more intuitive reporter than all the rest. I know because I am the dumb-ass that knocked on Jimmy's door the night before.

* * *

Two years and two Lombardi Trophies later, another spring day brings another gathering of media waiting for Jimmy Johnson. This time we are at a Delta gate at DFW Airport where Johnson is flying back from Pensacola, Fla.

The relationship between Johnson and owner Jerry Jones has reached the boiling point. Johnson and his assistant coaches' ignoring a toast from Jones at the NFL owners' meetings in Orlando, Fla., has led to Jones' famous "off the record" boast in a bar that 500 coaches could win Super Bowls for the Cowboys.

Johnson makes only the briefest remarks for the TV cameras gathered inside the terminal before he begins to choke up. Not one to show tears—this is after all a coach who yelled at a suffering player his first year in Dallas, "Asthma? The asthma field's over there!"—Johnson and girlfriend Rhonda Rookmaaker continue walking towards their car. A local camera crew will use footage that night, and for quite some time after, of *Morning News* columnist Frank Luksa and myself on each side of Jimmy, talking and walking away from the cameras.

Johnson is telling us he's willing to do an interview but not here with all the cameras gathered around.

I suggest that Rick Gosselin, our NFL writer that Johnson has known since his days at Oklahoma State, and Luksa and I meet him at his house in Valley Ranch.

Johnson, in a remarkable change from his stance of less than two years before, says that's fine, come on over.

About 30 minutes later, the three of us from the *Dallas Morning News* along with staff photographer David Woo are seated in Johnson's Valley Ranch living room. Johnson's parents, now in their 70s, have driven up from Port Arthur on the Texas coast to be with their son in these difficult but mostly just puzzling times. Johnson called them from the NFL owners meetings when the shit with Jerry started to fly in Orlando, knowing that this spat had gone way beyond the normal boundaries.

The elderly Johnsons make small talk with reporters before Jimmy, now having changed into his trademark "home" uniform of gym shorts and a T-shirt, enters the room.

Johnson isn't one for sitting still and engaging in small talk even when he's in the best of moods, but his mood is growing darker by the minute. He's getting angrier and angrier while scrubbing a giant fish tank in the corner of the room.

He is shouting to no one in particular. Soon, there are tears running down his face as he scrubs harder and harder to clean the saltwater tank. If this is an act, it's a sensational one.

"The cocksucker is taking my team away from me," Johnson yells. "I'm sorry, Mama."

It is one of the most uncomfortable scenes I have ever witnessed. I also know it's the place that every reporter and columnist covering the NFL at that very moment would have wanted to be.

Why am I there? In a two-year span, how did I go from being the butt of a private joke about reporters never knocking on Jimmy's door to having a front-row seat to a private meltdown in the living room of the reigning Super Bowl coach?

Being a good, industrious reporter? That's a small part of it.

Drinking many, many beers with Jimmy during that two-year stretch? Big, big part of it.

* * *

In 1992, with the Cowboys coming off of their first playoff win since the ownership change, the *Morning News* flipped assignments for several writers. This happened a lot in the '80s and '90s when sports staffs were growing and competing and constantly evolving.

Gosselin, who had covered the team the last two years but had more NFL sources than I could collect in a lifetime, moved to the NFL beat where I had been the last two seasons. I returned to the Cowboys beat and was joined by Ed Werder, who had covered the Cowboys in 1989 for the *Fort Worth Star-Telegram* before leaving for *The National*, Frank DeFord's fabulous but ill-conceived concept of a national sports section.

Johnson knew me well enough to say hello when we occasionally ran into each other around Valley Ranch. I had first met him when I had the briefest of stays—one bowl game and an off-season—on the Oklahoma State beat a decade earlier.

Actually, that's not totally true. The first time I ever spoke to him I was still the "statewide" high school writer for the *Daily Oklahoman*. Johnson had called the newspaper to speak to the person in charge of picking the all-state team.

When he was connected with me, Johnson informed me that his son, Brent, a linebacker, deserved a place on the team and that it would be a real disappointment and, frankly, an embarrassment for the newspaper if his son was not selected.

I knew his son was a good player and I had received some mention of him from coaches in the state but probably not enough to merit all-state.

I caved. I put him on the team.

In 1992, in addition to writing about the Cowboys on a daily basis, my job included a weekly appearance on Johnson's Ch. 4 coach's show. The show was taped on Thursday nights in downtown Dallas. Among other things, it was my first indication that the notion of NFL head coaches working impossible hours, maybe even doing the Joe Gibbs sleeping-on-an-office couch thing, was bullshit.

At least they were for one of the best young coaches who just happened to be dominating the NFL.

We had to be in a studio in downtown Dallas at 7 p.m. each Thursday. That's about a 25-minute drive from Valley Ranch because it's largely against commuter traffic. Johnson was always on time, waiting, and I was invariably pushing it right to the edge.

And that seemed strange to me.

How come I'm always cutting it close while writing about this team but Johnson has no problem being on time—and he's the coaching genius of this team?

Almost 20 years later, I don't recall anything groundbreaking about my segment in which I commented on some aspect of the team and asked Johnson a question. It's not like I compiled a resume tape, sent it to ESPN a decade later where some producer said, "That's our man!"

It was your basic bullshit coach's show. But one unexpected perk developed over time.

When we finished taping around 8 each week, Johnson and Rhonda would go to an On The Border restaurant in Dallas' West End area a few blocks away to sit at the bar, have a few drinks and usually watch college football if ESPN was showing a game.

A few weeks into the first season, Johnson asked if I wanted to meet them. I said of course.

For parts of that season and then almost every Thursday night during the 1993 season, the three of us would go to On the Border. We would drink beers and talk. The fact that it was off-the-record was never technically discussed. We both understood that this was just talk, nothing more than background information. If I had ever whipped out a notepad or tape recorder, the discussion would have ended and the relationship would have dissolved.

As time went by, Rhonda even told me one night, "This has been an awful week for Jimmy. He's really been looking forward to just coming here and hanging out with you."

Even 20 years later, typing that last sentence just feels strange but I promise you she said it.

Sometimes we would talk about the Cowboys or the NFL. More often we would talk about the college game and Johnson would tell stories, "the kind I can't put in my book," he would say.

One Thursday night in November, 1992, we met after the Cowboys had suffered an unexpected loss at home to the Los Angeles Rams. Troy Aikman had come under criticism—as much criticism as a young rifle-armed quarterback of an 8-2 team was likely to receive—for not risking an interception and throwing the ball in the end zone on the final play of a 27-23 defeat.

This was one of those times where we did talk Cowboys. I expected Johnson to defend Aikman after some columnists—Dallas did not have a radio sports talk station in 1992—had fired shots at him.

Instead, Johnson told me, "I understand what we have at quarterback. I know Troy's not John Elway. It's OK. We can win Super Bowls with what we have."

(By the time Aikman had won his third Super Bowl, prior to Elway collecting either of his two trophies, I didn't get to ask Johnson what he had thought. He was headed for the Dolphins and I was covering hockey.)

I didn't know then and I can't tell you today if this was just Jimmy's way of pumping himself up or if he still harbored serious doubts about Aikman two months before the team would win its first Super Bowl of the '90s. Maybe, just maybe Jimmy really had believed in 1989 that his former Miami quarterback Steve Walsh would make a better NFL quarterback than Aikman.

That was the kind of information I could store and use later, if possible. But mostly on these Thursday night beerfests—he always drank Heinekens, I drank a variety of Mexican beers—I learned that the one thing Jimmy really believed in was Jimmy.

One night in 1992 after several beers, he told me, "I never doubt that we are going to win Super Bowls here." I challenged him, saying that this little team in San Francisco with Steve Young and Jerry Rice and Ricky Watters was still pretty damn good and was going to be awfully tough to beat at Candlestick Park in the playoffs.

That's when Jimmy did his smacking-his-lips thing as if he can't believe he even has to answer such dumb questions.

"We are going to win Super Bowls," Jimmy told me, nodding his head. "Plural."

The cockiness that he was showing me that night would be in evidence for the football world a year later when, as defending champions, Johnson called Randy Galloway's local radio show before the 49ers rematch and said, "Put it in three-inch headlines. The Cowboys will win the game."

For a long time, people asked me if I thought Johnson had been drinking or "enjoying a few beverages" in his words when he made that prediction. The answer, of course, was yes. It was a Thursday night, and we just didn't have a TV show to tape during the playoffs. Otherwise, I would have been there with him!

I also learned that Jimmy's distrust of Jerry was genuine. I don't think he disliked him. Not yet, anyway. But at the time, Jimmy was frustrated with the fact that, having bailed him out of what would have been an expensive divorce, Jerry now had Jimmy over the barrel with his 10-year contract.

What had initially sounded like an over-the-top salary for an NFL coach—10 years, $10 million in 1989—now kept Jimmy from earning what a Super Bowl champion was worth. The ancillary benefits like the coach's show on Ch. 4?

Those checks ended up in Jerry's pocket.

And while Jimmy was invariably polite to the occasional fan that would venture over to the bar and ask for an autograph, I found out that the worst way to approach Jimmy (other than maybe knocking on his door) was to say, "Hey, I'm from Arkansas, too."

Jimmy's regular response (you have to nod your head and smack lips between each sentence for full Jimmy effect): "I'm from Port Arthur. I played football at Arkansas. I'm not FROM Arkansas."

* * *

And, yes, one of the things we joked about on those Thursday nights that first season was my having knocked on his door back in the spring. Jimmy loved to either hear my description or Rhonda's take on his reaction to seeing a reporter on his Valley Ranch doorstep.

Long story short: In 1992, the NFL's release of the Cowboys' schedule was a big deal in Dallas. It still is, of course, as the league has turned it into a prime-time show. Back then, the league sent out memos to the teams the day before it was officially released. It was a chance for teams to suggest changes in kickoff times if necessary but that was about it. The schedule was the schedule.

In those days before ESPN had a reporter in every town, it was a battle between the *Morning News* and the *Fort Worth Star-Telegram* to get the schedule. If you were the Cowboys beat writer working for Dave Smith, one of the most successful but demanding sports editors of his era, you did not want to wake up and see the Cowboys' schedule on the front page of the rival paper.

I got a call one spring evening about 6 p.m. from someone in the Cowboys' public relations office, saying he was pretty sure they had seen the coaches looking at the schedule that afternoon.

Oh—shit.

I found out quickly that Jerry was out of town and might not have seen it himself. The only way to get the schedule was to ask Jimmy.

Unlike Tom Landry, whose home phone number had always been available to reporters even if you couldn't expect a long conversation, no reporters had a home phone number for Jimmy. But I knew where he lived and, although we had not yet developed the beer-fueled bond that would come that fall, we had occasionally made jokes about having houses in the same neighborhood.

Someone was living beyond his means and someone else was living beneath his.

I told my wife that I thought I had to go knock on Jimmy's door. It wasn't a good idea but it was all I had.

It was about a 10-minute walk. Somehow I thought arriving on foot would seem more neighborly, less obtrusive than just pulling up in my car.

It felt like walking to prison.

(Let me rephrase and say it was like what I assume a walk to prison feels like. From first-hand experience, I can only tell you about jail).

When I arrived, Rhonda answered the door. She didn't know me at the time, so I told her what I was there for. She only had the door open a crack, poking her head out. She said she thought this was a bad idea.

I said I knew that, but I needed her to ask Jimmy if he would just come talk to me. If he said no, that would be it and I would leave.

A long minute or so later, the door opened wide. Jimmy, standing tall (for him) in gray gym shorts and shirtless, looked madder than I had ever seen him on the sidelines. He asked what I thought I was doing there.

I said, "I know the NFL schedule came out today and I didn't get it while I was out there and I need to see if you can give it to me for the paper tomorrow."

Johnson's reply: "And you thought it was a good idea just to knock on my door?"

I said, "No, I thought it was a bad idea but I don't have your home phone like I had Landry's."

Johnson: "That's right. And you'll never have it. You have just made a big mistake."

Slam.

Even now, I can hear Jimmy laughing, just thinking of this story.

But like any relationship between a reporter and the public figure that they cover, there were rocky times. I felt like Jimmy gave me a lot of good stuff off the record or after the fact on a story, but not enough when it counted. Meanwhile, it was clear to all of us at the *News* (and even more clear to Jimmy) that Jerry was giving inside information on a regular basis to Mike Fisher, the beat writer at the *Star-Telegram*.

While that frustrated me, Jimmy thought I owed him more than he owed me. And that came to a head—in the silliest of ways—in the 1993 season after the Cowboys had beaten the 49ers, 26-17, at Texas Stadium to raise their record to 4-2.

One of the beat writer's jobs for the Sunday paper was to give check marks to the Cowboys or their opponents in each week's matchups: Offense, defense, special teams, etc. Coaching also was included.

It got a little boring giving the Cowboys the coaching check mark week after week, but it was hard to avoid. They were the Super Bowl champs and the only reason they lost their first two games was Jones' unwillingness to give in to Emmitt Smith on his contract holdout.

So when the 49ers came to town, I was more than happy to acknowledge the presence of George Seifert, who owned the NFL's best winning percentage at the time.

Check mark, 49ers coach.

After Johnson's post-game press conference, he came down from the podium and headed for the door back to the Cowboys locker room. He stopped when he saw me. His mood just minutes after a huge win against the only team that could even play at the Cowboys' level turned sour.

"I saw what you did this morning," he said, shaking his head. "Giving the check mark to Seiftert…"

I said that both coaches had won a Super Bowl and that Seifert had the best record in the league.

"Yeah," he snapped. "He won a Super Bowl with Walsh's players. I won a Super Bowl with MY players. Keep this up, and I'll start giving my good stuff to Fisher."

Johnson turned to pass through the door to the locker room just as Aikman was walking in. "You see what he did today?" Johnson said to his quarterback. "Gave the check mark to Seifert."

Aikman looked at me, then looked at his coach who had moved on, headed back into his own little world. All Aikman could do was shake his head.

* * *

By the time the Cowboys were on the brink of winning their second Super Bowl under Johnson in Atlanta, I had a sense that something was up between Jimmy and Jerry.

Call it a sixth sense. Call it great reporting instincts.

Or call it the fact that a friend of Jimmy's told me that the coach's Corvette was in the team hotel's parking lot in Atlanta and that Jimmy was driving it to his new house in south Florida as soon as the Super Bowl ended.

Naturally, Jimmy managed to downplay the presence of the car when I asked about it. Yes, he had bought some property in the Keys and he was going down there for a while after the Super Bowl just to relax. No big deal.

But weeks went by and Jimmy was never seen around Valley Ranch.

One day in March he finally had returned, and I ran into Jimmy and Rhonda sitting in his other Corvette (he always kept two) at a convenience store in Valley Ranch. I asked about the draft.

"Shit, I haven't looked at a single tape," Johnson said. Then he started talking about Jacksonville and how pissed he was. "I had to tell Wayne Weaver to go ahead and hire (Tom) Coughlin because I can't get out of my contract," he said.

Now I was what we in Texas tend to call "kinda fucked." Jimmy was stretching the boundaries of the off-the-record stuff he would tell me after the fact. I had believed the Johnson-to-Jacksonville rumors at the end of the season were primarily Jimmy's attempt to get more money out of Jerry. I hadn't thought, despite the numerous hints he had given, he really, really wanted to go.

NOTE TO READERS: If the one thing you get out of this entire book is not only did I have a serious drinking problem but that I had a serious REPORTING problem, be my guest. I readily acknowledge in hindsight I whiffed at a lot of pitches that Jimmy left hanging out over home plate.

Even as I accumulated evidence that Jimmy had no desire to coach another minute for the Cowboys, I figured that when Jimmy went to the NFL owners' meetings in Orlando the next week that the juices would start flowing.

After all, nobody had ever coached three straight Super Bowl champions. Not Don Shula or Chuck Noll or Bill Walsh or even the man Johnson had so admirably replaced, Tom Landry. Another Super Bowl trophy would give him more than the man who had coached the Cowboys their first 29 years.

That had to be enough to fuel Jimmy's ego for the 1994 season, didn't it?

Besides, I was scheduled to fly to Los Angles to cover NCAA tournament games that coming week. I had been a fan of the tournament long before it became a national phenomenon known as March Madness. In the '70s in college, no one I knew filled out brackets. But a friend and I would draft the entire board and bet beers on the outcome of each game.

First-round games were one beer. Second-round games were two. The championship was a six-pack.

Drinking and sports? Yeah, you might say there has been a direct connection throughout my life.

So I wanted a little break from the Cowboys. It was the off-season after two long seasons of covering Super Bowl championships. I deserved as much.

Let Gosselin and Werder go to Orlando to cover the boring NFL owners' meetings. What the hell could possibly happen there?

* * *

Published: March 23, 1994

COWBOYS' JOHNSON WEIGHS FUTURE AS JONES MAKES, RETRACTS FIRING THREAT

By Ed Werder, Rick Gosselin

Staff Writers of *The News*

ORLANDO, Fla.-Jimmy Johnson said he is reconsidering his future as coach of the Super Bowl champion Dallas Cowboys after learning that team owner Jerry Jones made repeated threats about firing him early Tuesday morning.

Mr. Johnson confronted Mr. Jones with his concerns in a midday meeting. "I met with Jerry, and I'm still coach of the Cowboys," he said later. "This particular incident makes me pull back and reassess things."

Mr. Johnson abruptly left the NFL's annual spring meetings two days before their scheduled conclusion. He will miss his principal media commitment—a Wednesday morning coaches' breakfast.

"I've heard from numerous reliable sources that he was in the bar in the early hours of the morning and threatened to fire me, and said he was going to fire me at least eight or nine times," Mr. Johnson said. "I am really dumbfounded for the simple reason I don't know what I did."

Mr. Jones conceded that he made the remarks in an off-the-record forum, but he later insisted that he is not considering replacing Mr. Johnson, who has a chance this season to become the first NFL coach to win three consecutive Super Bowls.

"We've got a very good working relationship that withstands any of these personal differences or some of the frailties of being in a pretty highly visible situation," Mr.

Jones said. "I feel good about what we're going to be doing here in 1994, and I feel good about him coaching the Dallas Cowboys."

* * *

Incredibly, riding the high of consecutive Super Bowl victories, Jones and Johnson would end up parting ways a week later. How it all went down is an illustration of how different the news-gathering process is today but also how a little alcohol-driven bar talk can alter jobs and lives and the fortunes of entire franchises.

After Jones felt his toast was ignored by Johnson and former Cowboys assistants, he retreated to a bar at the resort hotel, accompanied by the team's personnel director Larry Lacewell. A number of writers were in the same bar, and they saw Jones accidentally knock over a lamp as he drank deeper into the right.

When some of the writers got up to leave, Jones grabbed Werder by the leg as he walked past. Jones had chastised Werder earlier in the night for his critical reporting of the owner's handling of the Emmitt Smith holdout that season.

"Don't leave now, you'll miss the story of the year," Jones told him. Werder asked what that might that be.

"I'm gonna fire our mother-fucking head coach," Jones said.

Needless to say, Werder, Gosselin and a few other writers decided to stay just a bit longer.

* * *

It was not unusual to hear Jones take playful shots at his head coach, just as it was customary for Johnson to rag on the team's owner on our Thursday night forays to On the Border.

If ever there was an accurate description of love-hate relationship, it was theirs. And as we would learn years later, while both were feeling on top of the world in the spring of 1994, owners of two Super Bowl rings each after just five years in the league, they would never duplicate this kind of success without each other's support.

Mention Jones' success as an owner to Johnson and you would most often get a roll of the eyes and an, "Oh, please…"

Jones had become increasingly mocking of Johnson as the accolades for the head coach rolled in. It was late in the evening, actually the early morning hours, back at the Cowboys team hotel after the team's 30-13 Super Bowl win over Buffalo when Werder and I made a brief appearance at a team party hosted by Jones.

Since the rumors about Johnson seeking the Jacksonville job had never been completely squashed, there was at least speculation that this might have been Jimmy's last game with Dallas.

When we congratulated Jones, one of us—I'm guessing Werder—said, "All you need to do now is keep your head coach."

Jones wasn't surprised that we would bring it up, only that we had it backwards.

"Maybe he needs to think about keeping his job here," Jones said.

This wasn't something to rush off and report. This was something said as a joke and with a smile and with a drink in hand. This was just Jerry being Jerry. It wasn't going to amount to anything the night of a Super Bowl victory.

But what was going on at a hotel bar in Orlando at the owners' meetings two months later? This was different. Jones wasn't just a little bit mad. Jones was tired of being pissed on publicly by Johnson. And the thing that Jones knew that those of us in the media did not was—whatever else you choose to say about him—this was a man who had the balls to do something about it.

As the angry words rolled off Jones' tongue, Werder and Gosselin surveyed the crowd. You have to understand this was a totally different era for newspaper reporters. After midnight was after deadline. There was nothing to write, no Internet monster to feed.

The *Morning News* writers knew there was a big story right here but it was just beyond their grasp. And at least two of the reporters for other newspapers that had wandered in and out of this strange scene had afternoon editions.

Not getting "the story of the year" was one thing. Getting scooped on it by writers who had mingled their way into a discussion that Jerry had intended for Dallas reporters was far worse.

At some point, Werder convinced Jones to meet with just the two of them the next morning and review the situation with Jimmy. Jones agreed. The things that had been said after many drinks were to be considered "off the record" but the owner made it clear he would not back off on what he had said. Werder and Gosselin went to bed, believing they had held off the other media members and that Jones would be true to his word and repeat his contention that 500 coaches could have won a Super Bowl with the Cowboys' talent.

Needless to say, the next morning before they ever spoke to Jones, all hell was breaking loose at the owners' meetings.

Lacewell, who had coached with Johnson in Oklahoma as far back as the '60s, had run into the head coach that morning. He warned Johnson of the things that Jones had said after having his toast ignored by Johnson and the other coaches.

Johnson was incensed. But he also knew this might present an opportunity to get out of what he now considered a demeaning contract in Dallas. It was too late to get the Jacksonville job but Johnson knew there would be no shortage of opportunities while he kept an eye on his ultimate goal of replacing Don Shula in Miami.

Jones, meanwhile, tried to sugarcoat his remarks from the night before. He was now hiding behind the "off the record" nature of his remarks and refusing to revisit his issues with Johnson as he had promised Werder and Gosselin.

That's how Johnson ended up being quoted more heavily in the above story than Jones, even though it was a creation of the owner's outburst to writers at the bar.

Jones started the ball rolling on the improbable notion of an owner getting rid of a head coach who had just won back-to-back Super Bowls. Now it was Jimmy's turn to run with it.

And that's how, a few days later, I found myself with a front-row seat to Jimmy's "The Cocksucker is Taking My Team From Me" show in his Valley Ranch living room.

* * *

Johnson could barely control himself once the tears started flowing that Saturday afternoon. I'm not sure what would have happened if his parents hadn't been seated 10 feet away. He tried to compose himself and said, "OK, let's do this interview," but I didn't think he was ready to do anything but get it over with and get us out of there.

About this time, Rhonda entered the room with nachos for everyone (I'm not making this up) and suggested, "How about some beers?"

For a thousand reasons, that seemed like a great idea. Thank God for Rhonda Rookmaaker.

Gosselin, Luksa and I spent the next two hours drinking Heinekens and watching Johnson regain his composure. We eventually got the interview from Johnson, candid and brutally honest, that no one could get that day in Dallas.

Since "cocksucker" was not an acceptable word for the Sunday paper, that quote never quite made it into print. Until now.

Still, it was incredible for a man who had left Dallas for the owners' meetings as the reigning king of the NFL to come home, saying this about what it would mean to be the first coach to win three straight Super Bowls:

"Right now with Jerry Jones as the owner—not a whole lot. I don't know how anybody could expect me to respect or trust a person such as that."

I should mention here that no one was getting drunk at Jimmy's house that Saturday afternoon. Sipping two or three, maybe even four beers over a long afternoon hardly seemed out of character for the time. And none of the other writers mentioned here qualify as serious drinkers.

Gosselin will drink a few beers now and then, but that's it. Werder, who wasn't at Jimmy's house anyway because he had been tracking him in Florida earlier that day, doesn't drink beer. He was constantly appalled to find himself stuck with me at beer-only establishments in Austin when the Cowboys trained there. Put an umbrella and a chunk of fruit in a colorful drink, and Werder will have a go at it. But his inability or unwillingness to drink Heinekens would have made him a poor candidate for a front-row seat at Jimmy's that day.

However, Werder had actually interviewed Johnson earlier that day in Pensacola, Fla., where Johnson had kept a promise—despite the unexpected developments at the owner's meetings—to appear at Emmitt Smith's football camp.

By Saturday night, Gosselin, Werder and I were all downtown at the *Morning News* office, relaying Johnson's comments to Jones on the phone as this high-stakes game of "He Said, He Said" played on.

When we told him what Johnson said about no longer trusting the owner, Jones said trust was a two-way street. "I also have the capacity not to trust or respect someone. Those feelings are not unique to Jimmy. That's the reason people quit working together."

Knowing now what I didn't know then—it takes years of being around Jerry and really listening to what he says to read between the lines—that's when it was over.

"That's the reason people quit working together," wasn't just an explanation of how Jones views the world. He was telling us what was about to happen although, coming off of two Super Bowl wins, it still seemed too crazy.

And three days later, it was over.

In the phoniest press conference I have ever witnessed, Johnson and Jones sat side by side and talked about how strong their relationship was now and why it was best to part ways.

Jones was barely 24 hours away from introducing Barry Switzer, a coach who wouldn't dream of stealing credit away from the owner. Nor would he deserve much.

Johnson had a $2 million check in his pocket. Dallas was just a few hours from being a place in his rearview mirror, one he would not visit unless required by Fox. Life in his beloved south Florida was about to begin.

* * *

In 2006, when the Mavericks played the Miami Heat in the NBA Finals, I drove down to the Keys on the Friday between Game 4 and Sunday's Game 5. I even called Jimmy on his cell phone. And, yes, I made it in the front door of the house without being told that I "had just made a big mistake."

And we drank a lot of beers that night and again the next morning while catching absolutely no fish. He blamed it on me for wanting to get out of bed at 8 instead of 5.

I was a lot more interested in drinking than fishing.

But drinking with Jimmy had helped me build a relationship that would be critical when it came to covering the biggest story of my life as a *Morning News* beat writer.

What would it have been like in 1992 to try to hang out with Jimmy and not have a single drink? Would he have developed any sense of trust with someone sitting there at the On the Border bar matching each of his Heinekens with a Diet Coke?

I have serious doubts. But it's not something I ever thought about until the spring of 2009.

(A Cowboys fan might ask another question: If not for heavy drinking in Orlando, would Johnson have remained as coach and won more Super Bowls for Dallas?)

But drinking with Jimmy—that was good times.

What could ever make me want to do away with that?

I don't know. I didn't stop to find out.

CHAPTER 5

SON OF WILLIS

"Oklahoma looked like hell. The land was black and charred. The air was full of smoke, the smell putrid."

—*The Worst Hard Time* by Timothy Egan

FOR BETTER OR worse, I remember almost everything in terms of what was going on in the sports world. I say almost everything because of one notable exception. First night I got laid?

July 29, 1974—the night Mama Cass of the Mamas and Papas died, eating a sandwich.

Don't even ask.

Everything else feels like it's tied to sports somehow. The time I spent a week in the hospital in fifth grade following a near-fatal asthma attack in which my boy scout brother, Pat, gave me CPR?

That's the Dodgers-Twins World Series. First six games of it, anyway. I was home for Game 7, then, alas, had to go back to being a normal kid who attends school.

The day Saddam Hussein was captured hiding down in that hole? Too easy. Dec. 14, 2003—the day Terence Newman intercepted three Redskins passes as a rookie.

How about my honeymoon with Lori in St. Thomas? February, 1987—when SMU got the death penalty.

Or the really important stuff like the night I scored 32 points in an intramural game at the University of Texas—that was March 28, 1977. I know that only because I recall it was a couple of hours before we all watched Al McGuire's last game, Marquette's national championship win over North Carolina.

The ability to link memories in this arcane manner has mostly limited value. I save a few minutes not having to look up dates or years from time to time, but that's about it.

The Phillies-Blue Jays World Series of 1993 itself is not a particularly memorable one for me. I did not cover it and had no emotional (or financial) stake in either team. I remember maybe feeling sorry for former Ranger Mitch Williams as Joe Carter tried to drive one of his pitches into the Skydome hotel in left field, but that's all.

That's it except before one of the games I recall stopping by my parents' north Dallas home to pick up something I had recently left behind and seeing a book next by my father's regular chair in the living room.

It was called *One Day at a Time*, and I didn't for a moment think it was likely to be a look back at Valerie Bertinelli's sitcom work. I knew it was a book read by people that went to Alcoholics Anonymous meetings.

I made the logical assumption. My father had bought it, intending to give it to me while making one of his speeches on the subject soon.

Sure enough, when I got home later that day, there was a message on my answering machine from my dad saying that he knew I was really busy covering the Cowboys but wondering if we could meet for lunch one day soon.

I racked my brain couldn't come up with any recent incidents that were leading my dad to make this assumption that I needed help. Clearly, he knew I drank beer and a lot of it. That happened just about any time we got together, even at the end of a round of golf, but he usually had a couple with me, and it had been years since I had come stumbling into the house after one too many.

But this was the conclusion I could make. It doesn't matter that I was 38, successful in my job, father of one child with another soon on the way. This was going right back to the old days of him on one side of the big desk and me on the other.

My dad was about to tell me I needed to go to AA. Who knows, maybe he even had an intervention lined up.

To understand why it couldn't be anything else, you need to know a little more about the life of Willis Ray Cowlishaw.

* * *

It began in Wolco, Oklahoma and if you Google Wolco, Oklahoma, you will learn absolutely nothing about it. A creation of the Wolverine Oil Company, its usefulness and its very existence were short-lived.

The Cowlishaw family tree came out of Wales in the 19th century and, thanks to the craftiness of one stowaway, crossed the Atlantic and made its way to Missouri. Willis' father, Ray, arrived in Avant, Oklahoma, with a team of mules brought down from Missouri in the early 1920s. At a boarding house in Avant, Ray became friendly with one of the women working there. He and Grace Thompson would eventually marry and move to Wolco where his team of mules landed him a job with the oil company. Soon the mules would be replaced by trucks as Wolco slowly crept up on modernity.

On June 18, 1926, Willis would be the first of five children born to Ray and Grace Cowlishaw. Four of the siblings would live long, productive lives but little Willard died early of whooping cough. Any mention of this still draws reluctant chuckles from my kids and their cousins, not because they are evil, uncaring people but because who in the 21st century has even heard of whooping cough?

When Wolverine sold to Shell in the '30s, company housing was no longer an option. Ray could keep his job but he had to choose between the more established communities of Skiatook or Barnsdall. And that is how a wonderful old house on a corner lot across from the old Skiatook High School became the site of so many Cowlishaw Christmases and family vacations into the late '70s when Grace, who had lived alone after Ray's death in 1944, finally relented to a nursing home.

Were times a little different in Skiatook back then? I guess you could say that. Kids today are reluctant to ride buses to school. Willis *drove* the school bus when he was in high school.

"I had been driving a truck for Greenwood's to deliver seed," Willis said. "It was a general store. We had a mill where we would grind the corn, and I'd take it out to the farmers in a truck. But I could drive the family car, too, an old '37 Pontiac with retread tries.

"The guy at school checked with Mr. Owens, my boss at Greenwood's, about my driving and gave me the job. The man who'd been driving it had just been drafted. They were taking everybody they could. I'll never forget there was a governor on the school buses, a board beneath the accelerator, and you could only go 35 miles an hour. Everything was rationed. We had gas stamps, and if you go slow, you burn less gas.

"My problem was the dirt roads. If it was raining, I couldn't spin the wheels enough to get them out of the mud. I'd have to have the kids come out into the road because if I pulled over to the side, I could get stuck."

Drinking and driving or driving while hung over was never a problem for young Willis. There was no liquor in the Cowlishaw household. Neither Ray nor Grace drank, and Willis was aware of it but did not partake.

"You have to remember I grew up in dry Oklahoma. The whiskey came in a brown paper bag from bootleggers who brought it down from Joplin. They would deliver it to your home. They had Three Feathers and Four Roses, cheap bourbon. Some of the brave guys drank it," Willis said. "I never did."

In the fall of '43, his senior year, Willis was like other kids (the bus-driving gig aside). He wasn't preparing for college, he was preparing for war.

"We wanted to be in the Navy; we didn't want any part of the army."

I'm not sure how a bunch of kids in land-locked Oklahoma knew that the naval life was the way to go, but they were mostly proved correct. "One of our guys, Billy Hasty, he didn't sign up with us. He waited 'til the Army got him. He was killed on D-Day plus two."

After graduation, Willis took the train from Tulsa to San Diego and went through gunnery school. From there he was transported to the Solomon Islands as one of the thousands of replacement troops for the battle in the Pacific. He was assigned to the USS Essex which was in the Philippines at the time. As a gunner's mate on the aircraft carrier, he survived a Kamikaze attack that killed 15 men and weathered three typhoons as the ship supported the attacks on Okinawa and Tokyo in the late stages of the war.

And then there was shore leave. No need for a designated driver at the time, Willis was more like a designated dragger or carrier.

"When the war was over, we came through the Panama Canal and they gave us liberty for four hours while they filled the locks with water," Willis said. "I remember going to a bar with a bunch of sailors. The guys were drinking with both hands as fast as they could. We hadn't been there an hour when one of the guys passed out. They gave him to me to get back to the Essex because I wasn't drinking."

*　*　*

After World War II, Willis married Wanda McDowell of Bartlesville, Okla., in October, 1946. Grace and Wanda's mother, Lola, had been friends since childhood. A post-Naval college education wasn't really in the cards, but Willis attended watchmakers' school at Hardin College in Wichita Falls, Tex.

Thus would begin an improbable journey of more than 30 years in the jewelry business, the last 28 within the ranks of the Zale Corporation as Willis scaled the corporate ladder to serve as President of the Fine Jewelers Guild representing more than 300 stores across the country and as far away as Guam.

After Pat was born in Muskogee in 1951 and I came along in Tulsa—big-city guy that I am—in 1955, this journey would land Willis and family in New Jersey in 1961.

You've heard of *A Tree Grows in Brooklyn*? How about *An Okie Runs Jewelry Stores in Newark*?

It was an education for him in many ways as well as those who worked for Willis.

Before there were malls, there were large jewelry stores in the heart of our nation's cities. So it was with Wiss Jewelers on Broad Street in Newark. It didn't take Willis long to figure out he wasn't in Oklahoma any more.

"The lady in charge of costume jewelry and handbags, Elvina Hockman, had 10 girls working for her in her department in the back of the store," Willis said. "We only had four or five girls up front and one day—I hadn't even been there a month—we got very busy and so I brought one of her girls up to the front. I was her boss. She was happy to do it.

"Well, when Elvina came back from lunch, she grabbed the girl and said, 'Don't ever come back up here.' She told me never to do that again. She gave me a lecture. She was belligerent.

"As soon as I got the right time, I took her to my office and said, 'Look. I'm running the store. If I need one of your employees, they may work in your department, but I'm going to take them up here.' Well, she said she wasn't happy about it. I told her she sounded like she'd been drinking, and she said, certainly, she always has a couple of martinis at lunch with her cheeseburger. She asked if I had some kind of objection to that.

"I said, 'Yes, you don't drink while you're working.' And she laughed in my face."

The next day Willis hung a sign on the bulletin board in the employees' break room that spelled out there was to be no drinking during store hours. That included no drinking during lunch breaks.

The store's former owner, Victor Paul, who had sold the business to Zale's, maintained an office on a balcony overlooking the store. The employees, or at least some of them, went to see him to complain the next day.

On Day Two of the no-drinking policy, Willis got a phone call to go up to see Victor Paul. He asked Willis what had prompted him to put up the sign. Willis said he had an argument with Elvina and could smell liquor on her breath.

Victor laughed and asked Willis if ever drank at lunch. Willis said no, that he rarely drank and if he did it was at home after store hours.

Victor said, "Well, I have a drink at lunch. You're in the East now, Willis. There are bars all over the place here. This isn't Oklahoma. I've got to tell you you're not right about this. You cannot tell your people not to drink at lunch."

The sign came down. Willis had lost his first battle with alcohol.

* * *

The years went by. We moved to Texas, lived in three different houses. I became old enough to drink beer with my dad on the golf course or have a glass of wine at the formal dinner table on a holiday or a special evening. But drinking at the dinner table on any regular night—that was not something he ever did. And he wasn't the type to have a drink at his side while watching TV late at night, either.

Yes, there was a liquor cabinet going back to my junior high days, but that was stocked mostly for the occasional party or bridge night. And those nights were rare.

Once my father remarried, there was always vodka in the house for Patricia, but that was something she sipped with her Rose's lime juice. Nobody in this house was getting hammered.

When it came to alcohol, the Cowlishaws of fashionable North Dallas weren't that far removed from Ray and Grace Cowlishaw of Skiatook.

While I managed to successfully hide my high school drinking, I did have occasional stumbles in front of the parents not too long after. I came home from Oklahoma City one night in October 1980 to attend—don't kill me here—a Cars concert at Reunion Arena.

And, yes, I can tell you the exact date if you like (Oct, 12, 1980) because I know it was the night of Game 5 of Astros-Phillies in the LCS. So, yeah, with the purchase of my first VCR still a year or two away (actually it was to be a Betamax and a first wedding present), I missed Nolan Ryan's famous 8th-inning meltdown that prevented Houston from its first World Series. All because I wanted to go see Ric Ocasek and the boys.

Probably a bad call all the way around.

Making matters worse, I was dropped off at my parents' house in a state in which I was unable to get the key in the door at 1 in the morning. Patricia had to let me in as I mumbled-stumbled my way to the guest bedroom.

When I awoke the next morning, I was told in no uncertain terms by Patricia that I was to go see my father in his office at 10 o'clock before driving back to Oklahoma City. Never mind that I had a job and needed to get to work.

His house. His rules.

It was not a pleasant visit. I sat on the wrong side of his massive desk at the old Zale Building off Stemmons Freeway and listened to him wonder aloud what I was hoping to accomplish in life, why I was out so late, why I drank so much, why I went to some concert when he thought I would want to watch the Astros in the playoffs for God's sake.

"What are your goals?" Willis asked.

At the time, my immediate goal was to slink out of the office, down the hall to the elevator, into my car and get out of town. Beyond that—much like Lloyd Dobler at the dinner table with his girlfriend's father in *Say Anything*—I knew mostly a bunch of things I didn't want to do or be, but I couldn't really figure it out just then.

* * *

So it had been 13 years since that meeting at Zale's, and there were no recent mumble-stumbles on my record. At least not to my dad's knowledge. Still, his invitation to lunch sounded ominous.

I thought of all the things I planned to tell him that I had accomplished as a reporter, as a father, as a productive adult. I decided I was willing to admit that I drank too much and that I was willing to work on it, maybe carve out some kind of plan to reduce my beer consumption (vodka was just arriving as a regular in my life in 1993 and no one outside the house was aware of it).

But I was going to draw the line when he brought up AA. I didn't need to go meet with a bunch of losers and hear their pathetic stories, and I certainly was in no mood to enlighten others with mine. I couldn't quite mimic Oklahoma State Coach Mike Gundy ("I'm a man, I'm 40!") but I was 38, dammit, and old enough to make these decisions for myself without any parenting interference.

And so one afternoon that week we met at Blue Mesa in north Dallas just east of the Tollway. Although I am ridiculously on time for things compared to most people, Willis is always early so he was waiting when I arrived. We shook hands when we met like rival captains at the 50-yard line. We were seated at a table in the middle of the room. We ordered iced teas. I started eating chips and salsa.

My father cleared his throat to speak.

"Tim, I've got something I need to tell you," he said. "Your father is an alcoholic."

CHAPTER 6

AND THEN THERE WAS HOCKEY

"In heaven there is no beer
That's why we drink it here.
And when we are gone from here
Our friends will be drinking all the beer."

—Soggy Bottom Boys from the movie
O Brother Where Art Thou?

TIME: November, 1995
PLACE: The Broadmoor Resort, Colorado Springs

THE MAN AT our table has stood up and instructed all of us—not just those of us at his table but everyone in the entire pub—to turn to a certain page in our songbooks. He will now lead us in song.

"Oh Danny Boy, the pipes, the pipes are calling
From glen to glen and down the mountain side…"

A big man, our lead singer does not have a booming baritone by any means. But he can carry a tune, and he is committed (as always) to getting the most out of his moment in the spotlight—his shift, if you will—and doing the best that he possibly can.

Who is this, you ask, and where exactly are we?

Excellent questions.

The leader in song is Bob Gainey, head coach and general manager of the Dallas Stars, an NHL team that is scuffling on the ice to collect wins and at the gate to attract fans to this almost anti-Texan sport in its third season since moving from Minnesota.

Gainey, a storied Hall of Fame player in Montreal, is in his sixth season on the job. After one of the most remarkable playoff runs in NHL history in his first season as a coach—the North Stars were a playoff-worst 27-39-14 but reached the Stanley Cup Finals against Pittsburgh—Gainey's teams have won only one playoff series in four years since.

But he isn't thinking about the difficulties of finding wings who can skate with speedy young center Mike Modano or convincing 6-foot-4, 225-pound defenseman Kevin Hatcher that it's OK to hit people once in a while or the task of selling hockey in a football state. Not right now, he isn't.

He's thinking about fighting his way through this first verse with the help of his bar mates.

> *"The summer's gone and all the roses falling,*
> *'Tis you, 'tis you must go and I must bide."*

The summer is, in fact, gone here at the Broadmoor Resort in Colorado Springs. It's early November, and the Stars are 15 games into another regular season that will end without a trip to the playoffs.

A team that is about as average as one can get—its unsettling 5-5-5 record indicates that the NHL has not yet adopted "shoot out" rules—has made a pit stop on this long season's journey to nowhere. After playing Colorado to a 1-1 tie on a Thursday night in old McNichols Arena, the Stars do not play again until Tuesday when they face Mario Lemieux in Pittsburgh. But rather than return to Dallas, Gainey has gathered players, scouts and even the organization's sports psychologist at this Colorado Springs resort for three days of meeting and focusing and team bonding—the kind of things NHL teams are more prone to do than their colleagues in other professional sports.

And this resort includes a popular little British pub called The Golden Bee in which, in addition to the traditional Shepherd's Pie and Fish and Chips on the menu, patrons are given songbooks for impromptu sing-a-longs.

And, oh yes, did I forget to mention the beer?

The beer at the Golden Bee is sold by the yard or, for the more timid or those less in need of thirst-quenching, half-yard.

And Gainey is into his second yard as are the two beat writers covering the Stars in what will be a mostly forgettable season—Mike Heika, in his second year on the beat for the *Fort Worth Star-Telegram*, and, yes, yours truly.

I came for the hockey. I stayed for the beer.

* * *

When Jimmy Johnson and Jerry Jones parted ways, I stayed one more season on the Cowboys' beat. It was an eventful year, to say the least, with Barry Switzer taking over more as summer camp director than head coach, but the team fell short of a third straight Super Bowl trip in a 38-28 NFC championship loss to San Francisco.

Troy Aikman's first pass in that title game was intercepted and returned for a touchdown, and there are thousands of Cowboys fans to this day who will tell you that it only happened because Switzer was (ostensibly) in charge, and that had Johnson stayed, such a crucial mistake would never get made.

It's a ridiculous point that has merit only if one can assume that Johnson would have somehow regained the motivation that he had exhausted with that second Super Bowl win and his subsequent efforts to get the hell out of Dallas and, if at all possible, to Miami or at least Jacksonville.

Beyond that, the 49ers with Steve Young and Jerry Rice and Ricky Watters and, for 1994, anyway, Deion Sanders—that was a really, really good team and at some point it was likely to break through the barrier and beat the Cowboys of Aikman and Smith and Irvin no matter who was on the Dallas sideline.

Regardless, even if the Cowboys were poised to rebound in 1995, I wasn't.

I turned 40 that year. My son was born that year. I was shifting into early mid-life crisis mode. After three straight years of covering the Cowboys—six total going back to 1986—I needed something different in my professional life.

You remember the 2004 Red Sox and their "Cowboy Up" mantra? I was, if I may invent a word, Cowboyed out. And that's despite the fact that we had bought a house in Valley Ranch less than a mile from the team's practice facility. Our address, as a matter of fact, was Cowboys Parkway.

The Stars beat came available. My hockey knowledge was limited to games I had watched as a kid when there was a Sunday afternoon game on CBS and to the many, many nights attending Dallas Blackhawks games during high school and trips home from college. They played at the old State Fair Coliseum near the Cotton Bowl. They even had 10-cent beer night. Yes, I attended.

People in the business would understand switching to a less prominent beat. Outsiders would think the Cowboys beat in Dallas or the Red Sox beat in Boston are the jobs that sportswriters aspire to. In some ways they are, but they're also the high-pressure gigs that drive people crazy. Or at least make them miserable. Spend a little time in the Yankees clubhouse—not around the players but the paranoid writers—and you'll see what I mean.

Everything the Cowboys do is big news. They don't have to be winning to make that happen although, my last three years on the beat, they were winning like they never had before. After a few years, it can wear you down.

I also had this notion that the more pro sports I could cover, the more valuable it made me in the long run. Either that would lead to a columnist job because of my versatility or it would increase my value to other newspapers.

So I switched beats. The other writers in Dallas, as I say, understood.

My parents? Not so understanding.

"You're going to cover who? The Dallas Stars?" they asked.

They thought I was about to get fired. I half-expected to hear another pitch from my dad about the jewelry business as I had coming out of college when he doubted my future in newspapers—except for the fact that his Zale's experience had ended badly on its own in 1983 when he was given a golden parachute that had a few holes in it.

So that's how I found myself seated at the Golden Bee, polishing off my first yard of beer and ready for another while trying to accompany Gainey's surprising tenor in the traditional Irish song.

Drinking with Jimmy had been replaced by Drinking with Bo (that's not a typo; Bob is Bo, especially after a couple of beers). There were few similarities.

For one, despite this unusually relaxing stay in Colorado Springs, the NHL tends to be three games a week, sometimes four, lots of hopping on planes for bad coach seats—the Stars were one of the last organizations to charter and had not reached that advanced stage in 1995-96.

In addition, Gainey, though fully aware of his need to be out front as a salesman for this sport in the Lone Star State, was not naturally drawn to that aspect of the job. While he was mostly accommodating to the media—which back then, on a daily basis, was me and Heika—going out for drinks to spill a few secrets to the writers was not high on Gainey's list.

Beyond that, Gainey's time as head coach was almost at an end. Within two months, he would step aside, limiting himself to the GM duties while promoting Ken Hitchcock to head coach. The move will turn out to be terrific for the team but it will also mean a lot less daily contact with the media for Gainey.

The Canadiens, it turns out, had stayed in Colorado Springs for a similar bonding experience during their Cup-winning days in the '70s. Gainey recalled watching *Monday Night Football* one night in the Busy Bee with his teammate Frank Mahovlich. "The Big M," that rarest of players to have won multiple Stanley Cups with both Toronto and Montreal, was finishing his NHL career with the Canadiens just as Gainey's was getting started. For reasons Gainey could not recall, Mahovlich was a big Los Angeles Rams fan. Or it's possible—one feels safe in assuming—that Mahovlich might have placed a small wager on the Rams for this particular Monday night contest.

The game did not go well for his team. Gainey remembered that late in the contest (and late in the evening), a customer walked into the Busy Bee and asked at their table how the game was going.

Mahovlich didn't even look up. "I've drank more yards than the Rams have gained," he said.

* * *

Gainey told other tales of drinking, of all-night poker games and of how one Canadien talked for days about his excitement to get to a favorite whorehouse in San Francisco, only to have players warn the owner of the house just before his arrival, "The guy coming to your door is an undercover cop."

Mostly, Gainey made the Canadiens sound like Paul Newman's Johnstown Chiefs of *Slap Shot* fame, at least off the ice. On the ice, they were simply the best hockey team on the planet and one of the greatest of all time.

Mahovlich, in fact, would go on to finish his career with the WHA's woeful Birmingham Bulls. A man who had played with the greatest in the game in Toronto, Detroit and Montreal actually skated on a line with one of the Hanson Brothers from *Slap Shot*.

In fact, the story goes that Mahovlich was asked what was wrong with the team after one of the Bulls' many defeats. "I don't know," he said, "I just seemed to play better with Howe and Delvecchio."

* * *

Although I would have beverages a few more times over the years with Gainey, I never again saw him in the story-telling mood he enjoyed that night in Colorado Spring. And yet I have wondered since about Gainey's choice of songs. I wasn't that familiar with *Danny Boy* at the time or at least did not realize how often it was sung at Irish wakes or memorial services. Gainey was less than five months from having buried his wife, Cathy, who died of brain cancer.

At a beautiful resort like the Broadmoor, an early snow falling on the lake outside the pub, it would seem natural for

Gainey to be thinking back on happier times while he's sharing drinks and stories with a couple of writers.

Or maybe he had just accumulated enough yardage in beer that it was time to sing that song.

Gainey is one of those athletic types who can not only drink a serious amount of beer without acquiring the body fat so familiar to the rest of us, he really doesn't even change demeanor, either. Where others struggle with their balance or their thoughts, Gainey keeps moving forward, as if transporting the puck down the ice away from the danger of his own net towards safety.

Forever making the most out of his shift.

* * *

The only drinking with Hitchcock, Gainey's successor behind the bench and the man so instrumental behind the improved play that would lead to a Stanley Cup, involved coffee. And I never drank coffee.

That's not to say I didn't get along with Hitch. I did and quite well. But it was a professional relationship untied to the cocktail hour.

For the three years I spent on the Stars beat, there were many post-game nights in bars in and around the team hotels. That's where writers such as *The Globe and Mail*'s Eric Duhatschek and Allan Maki or the *Toronto Star*'s Damien Cox or Stars front-office types like Craig Button or Doug Armstrong educated me and furthered my love for the good old hockey game.

I ask again, if I had been standing at the bar those nights with a Diet Coke in my hand, would I have developed the same friendships and relationships and had the same learning experiences that would make me a successful hockey beat writer and, using that as a springboard, the paper's lead columnist?

My guess is maybe I could have found a way to make it happen but it would have been more difficult. It would have involved me wanting to distance myself from the rest of the boys, and that wasn't something I was even remotely ready to address.

And so the Kokanee Gold flowed. And flowed.

CHAPTER 7

WILLIS SENDS A MESSAGE

"If learning is living and truth is a state of mind,
You'll find it's better at the end of the line."

—*Tear-Stained Eye* by Son Volt

THERE IS A downside to the surprise ending, even when the initial surprise has granted you considerable relief.

"*OK, so my dad's not going to get on me today about my drinking. It's all about him, not me. Damn, this adobe pie is good, and I need to take some of these chicken taquitos home with me...*"

The downside comes when the relief wears off and you realize that the guy who is addressing his drinking issues isn't the guy at the table with the more serious drinking problem.

My first thought: My dad and I can't drink a beer any more at the end of a round of golf. That's sad.

My second thought: Maybe he'll get over this. He'll go to a few AA meetings, he will realize that, generally speaking, the people there are way more fucked up than he is and he'll stop going. And he'll gradually drift back into having the occasional beer with me after kicking my ass in golf.

But as he talked about his problem—or what he considered to be his problem, saying things like "One night I drank so much that the next morning I couldn't remember how the night ended" to which I wanted to say "Once? This happened to you once?" —I knew he wasn't coming back to the land of the drunks. He had rarely ventured into our world, at least in my mind, and he saw nothing to be gained by going back.

I just kept thinking: When did he do all this clandestine drinking? We all saw him have a cocktail or two, but if he really had a problem, how did he hide it so well?

It would take me more than a decade to learn just how hereditary some things are between father and son.

* * *

My father was 67 years old when he went to his first AA meeting. That combined with the former Cowboys coach Jim Erkenbeck's suggestion he was going to quit at 65 bought me a considerable amount of time. I had about two good decades of drinking left.

Seriously, I thought of life in those terms, as ridiculous as that sounds. You know you have a problem, you know even if you aren't driving drunk and aren't slapping your wife and kids around that, at the very least, you are bound to be damaging your liver and destroying brain cells. And you tell yourself you are going to deal with it—in 20 years?

Kind of pathetic.

* * *

My parents lived a busy social life with Patricia being involved in all sorts of charity functions. Over time, I learned that she had been driving home from many of those events after Willis had too much to drink.

"She would tell me that I didn't walk that steady or that my voice had changed," he said. "I didn't argue and say, 'Give me the keys,' or any of that. I let her drive.

"There must have been several occasions where guys would ask me what I was talking about. I didn't understand. I was starting to get my stories mixed up. In October of '93, we had been to a party at Las Colinas that probably lasted until 1 o'clock. I had gone back and kept getting more scotches. I loved to dance as you know. It was after midnight.

"We went out to get the car. I sat on the curb, ringing wet from all the dancing. A man who lives down the street from us said, 'Willis, isn't it a god-damn shame the band quit playing? You were really having a good time tonight.'

"I tell that story in AA now. 'The band had quit playing.' That's how it was for me. It wasn't fun anymore."

My father received a golden parachute from Zale's in 1983. It was a parachute with all kinds of holes in it. The profit-sharing and much of the retirement income he thought would set him up for years to come was soon gone.

He could have had any number of jobs and his kids were grown and away from home, but he didn't want to leave Dallas. He spent years as a consultant, trying to drum up business in a jewelry industry that was changing and struggling. On road trips to cities where he would try to find buyers for small jewelry companies, he found himself alone at night, 60 years old, his future uncertain.

"I was never one to go to my hotel room and put on a movie," he said. "I went to the hotel bars. I sat by myself and drank."

Out of sight from his family, he developed an alcohol dependency. With Patricia back in Dallas, he would drink too much at parties. In 1993, it reached a head.

Sorry to spoil it for Robert Earl Keen fans, but the road does not, in fact, go on forever. The party does end. And the band stops playing.

On a Sunday morning in October, 1993, my dad went to his first AA meeting. He felt a little bit scared. He also felt a little bit above it all, like he didn't belong. It was a Sunday morning, so he wore a sports coat and nice slacks, the most casual attire he would ever consider wearing to church.

No one else at the meeting was dressed like him.

"There were old pickup trucks in the parking lot. There were guys in painters' uniforms in the room," he said. "A man came over and said, 'You're new here. Let's go over here and talk. Do you think you're an alcoholic?'

"I said, 'Oh, I don't think so. I just have hangovers and I'm starting to black out and not remember things.

"He said they had a test for alcoholics, and I said, 'Good, I like tests. What is it?'

"He said, 'What do you drink?' I said J & B Scotch.

"He said, 'OK. I want you to go home and I want you to get a shot glass. Drink one shot a day for 30 days, then come see me. You can't save them up and drink a bunch of them on Friday or Saturday.'

"I said, 'One shot a day? I drink doubles with a splash of water. I can't do that.'

"He showed me the 12 steps. I said I can't do those steps. He said, 'Well, are you just going to be a dry drunk? You'll be mad and we're a happy lot here.'

"I remember after the meeting there must have been 12 of us went to a Jo Jo's coffee shop. They had apple pie and ice cream, diet Cokes or whatever and they just laughed like crazy. I thought, 'What are these people so happy about? Nobody's got a drink.'"

My father has been going to AA meetings two or three times a week for 20 years. He has sponsored a number of people, some of them for years.

He's the one who's happy and laughing and telling stories now. He hasn't had a drink since 1993, and that doesn't bother him in the least.

"I don't think it was even three months until I found out I didn't even miss it," he said. "It was really just a relief for me. Drinking had become like work for me. I didn't have to do it anymore."

* * *

Willis never lost his love for golf during his drinking years. But once he moved into sobriety, his health improved and so did his game. A guy who shoots in the high 80s when he's in his 50s is just another golfer. A guy who shoots in the high 80s when he's in his 80s is something special.

I rarely work family members into my columns—my kids have made infrequent appearances—but in 2007 I wrote a column about a local golfer named Willis Ray. Family and friends knew who I was talking about. Others didn't know until the final paragraph that this column—about a golfer who shot his age (an 81 at 81)—was Willis Ray Cowlishaw.

He does it in spite of what one club pro, trying in vain to correct Willis' swing flaws, called "an educated lunge."

I call it the "constant parabola."

By any name, for the last 30 years, his tee shots have started off in the direction of the trees, the fence, the out-of-bounds stakes, whatever lies on the left side of the fairway. First-time viewers are wont to gasp, fearing a costly mistake has been made.

When the ball lands softly on the left-center of the fairway rolling gently towards the 150-yard pole in the middle, the shot is complete. And it is executed nearly to perfection, one par 4 or 5 after another. Each time, Willis says something like, "Didn't go anywhere."

He'll never understand. Those of us who hit the ball farther but have to make sure we have a solid inventory of balls in our bag before each round appreciate the value of the short but well-placed drive in the heart of the fairway.

Willis played no golf in the summer of 2010. Most of us assumed he would never play again and I'm sure he had similar thoughts although he didn't talk about it much. What started out as a hiatal hernia with considerable stomach and chest pain developed into heart surgery, infections and four months on his back in Dallas hospital beds.

We watched the U.S. Open golf from his hospital room. We watched Celtics-Lakers from his hospital room (usually just the first half, he would be asleep by halftime).

By the time he was able to go home and move slowly with a walker at home, he was an 85-year-old man with—no sternum. Without getting into all the medical details (in part because I don't truly understand them), the chest bones were so brittle that by the end, they just tied everything up with a net, patched him up and sent him on his way.

One of the doctors who worked with him on his rehab exercises in 2011 was Dr. Drew Dossett, the Cowboys' team orthopedist. When I saw him after a game that fall as he was headed to the locker room, Dossett stopped and said, "Your dad. Amazing. I asked his heart doctor how often he has had to send someone home without a sternum after surgery, and he said, 'Never. I just thought it would work for him.'"

Initially, Willis was told he could try some chipping and putting. Nothing strenuous. Heaven forbid no drivers.

At some point, he was instructed he could try to play holes from the 150-yard marker in to the green. I don't know. This sounds like something he might have made up, but who am I to tell an 85-year-old man what he may or may not have heard from his doctor?

So towards the end of 2011, my dad and brother and I drove to the Hill Country outside Austin and played two rounds at the Horseshoe Bay Resort course and then at a wonderful course called Comanche Trace in Kerrville.

Dad played the par 3s from the white tees. On the fours and fives, he dropped a ball at the 150-yard marker, counted it as his tee shot and finished the holes.

It was great to have him back out on the course. It was something we didn't even dare to consider as a possibility during the long hospital summer of 2010.

For Willis, it was less than satisfactory.

His rehab continued. His health improved. He lost weight.

He's still not hitting a driver, but he's swinging away from the white tees with those 3-and 4-woods. The "educated lunge" is back. The "constant parabola" is back.

At age 85, he shot an 89 yesterday at Twin Creeks Golf Course in Allen.

It is something approaching a medical miracle.

You want to see a guy smiling without a drink on his hand? That's my dad coming off the 18th green.

I see that now but I couldn't see that a decade ago when I was the new lead sports columnist for the *Dallas Morning News*. In the summer of 1998, I shot way out over my skis when I became the News' new lead sports columnist.

My life was like that scene from *Broadcast News* when William Hurt asks, "What do you do when your real life exceeds your dreams?"

Albert Brooks' response: "Keep it to yourself."

I was determined to enjoy my time as a columnist, work hard during the day and play hard whenever possible at night. And while I was thrilled to have a six-figure income for writing sports, in 2002, ESPN was about to double my income and change my life even further.

* * *

INTERLUDE

YOU MIGHT HAVE A DRINKING PROBLEM IF…

…You stop at the liquor store with your three-year-old daughter in the backseat. You take her in with you because, well, it's a heck of a lot better than leaving her in the car. You're not THAT guy, at least.

Plus you seem to recall this particular liquor store—just east of the "dry" Irving border on Northwest Highway—has candy suckers (Dum Dums, you believe) at the counter for kids, and you're pretty certain you have taken Rachel in there before and she enjoyed getting a sucker.

When you enter the store, she takes off running in front of you. She runs to the center aisle, turns right, runs past three rows of shelves, turns right again and reaches down to grab the plastic bottle of Gordon's Vodka on the bottom shelf.

You realize that yes, in fact, she has been there a few times before. Perhaps a few more times than you recall.

* * *

…Your daughter is 16 now. You are preparing to take her on a great trip to LA over spring break to visit UCLA and UC-Santa Barbara, just the two of you. She's not certain she can get into either school, you are even less certain you have stored away the necessary dollars to pay for this kind of out-of-state tuition, but you are both excited about the trip.

You've got a nice room reserved at the JW Marriott Le Merigot on Santa Monica's Ocean Ave.

But the night before the trip you have to confess something to her in your apartment. It has been eight months since your DWI and none of your immediate family members—wife, kids, parents, brother—know about your arrest. Renting cars can be a huge pain in the ass because of the form you have to produce in place of a driver's license, the piece of yellow paper that says you got a DWI but adds in big letters—as if this is totally reassuring to the confused rental car agent at the counter—THIS IS NOT AN ADMISSION OF GUILT.

"Hey, I just want a damn Sentra and I'm not going to wreck it, ok?"

Because of the potential for confusion and delay at the airport rental counter, you tell your daughter—tears in your eyes now—that you made a huge mistake eight months ago and had too much to drink and got pulled over and, no, you didn't hit anyone or wreck the car, you just had a little too much and, anyway, you got a DWI and sometimes it takes a while to rent a car but don't worry, we will get a car and the trip will all be OK.

Your daughter looks hurt but she does not cry. She hugs you.

She does not seem surprised.

* * *

…You're in California for Cowboys' training camp in the summer of 2008. The team practices in Oxnard but you stay in nearby Ventura, and it's the small but active bar scene in Ventura that is the highlight of training camp.

It's a morning practice and you are tired from the night before but don't feel especially hung over. You manage to get Jerry Jones off to the side to ask him about his 20th season as the team's owner and president. Before you can get your question out, Jones looks at you and, with a smile, says, "Tim, it looks to me like you've been hittin' Ventura a little too hard."

* * *

...You're at the ESPN party at the Super Bowl in Jacksonville. Alicia Keys is onstage but she isn't performing, she's just introducing some of the local rappers and R&B artists there. The music is good. The free drinks are flowing. You have quite a few.

Some of the black artists who have been on the stage or are getting ready to perform recognize you at the bar from *Around the Horn*. You hit it off. You talk sports, you talk music, you ramble about whatever comes to mind.

An hour or two passes. Before you know it, you are in a car with total strangers to go to some house where, supposedly, Alicia Keys is going to be. When you get out of the car, you don't really like the looks of the house. You are sober enough to harbor serious doubts that this is where Alicia Keys is likely to be staying.

As the others head into the house, you pull out your phone and say you will be in there in a second. You fake a phone conversation as they disappear inside.

You walk down the street of what's—let's say—a lower middle class neighborhood in Jacksonville. Furniture on a few front porches. Chain-link fences in the front yard.

You walk about a block and you see a couple of young black men talking in their front yard. You hope they recognize you, but they don't. You tell them you need to get a ride back downtown to the Westin, that you were with some friends out here who have decided to stay and you need to get back.

You tell them you've got $40 in your pocket for the ride.

They look skeptical about your story, but one of them goes inside to grab his keys.

They give you the ride back to the hotel. They say they don't need the money.

You go up to your room. It's about 3 a.m.

You are glad that Super Bowl kickoff the next day isn't until 6:30 because you are going to stay in bed until noon and wonder, just a little bit, about the hell just happened.

* * *

...You are at the Super Bowl in Detroit. Part of the *Dallas Morning News* contingent is downtown, but you and two others are out in Livonia, which (besides being the hometown of Dallas hockey icon Mike Modano) is a long drive from downtown where all the parties are taking place.

You spend more time behind the wheel than you would like—this is January, 2006, so you do not yet have a DWI on your record—but you survive the week without incident.

Mostly without incident.

On one particular night that you are driving another writer back from downtown, you get lost on the Michigan highways. Your co-worker isn't much help with the guidance. After driving an hour more than the 40-minute trip should have taken, you finally see the glow of the Marriott in the distance.

You pull into the parking lot. It doesn't look as familiar as you would like.

You approach the desk clerk. You ask him politely how to get to the Livonia Marriott.

He says, "Livonia? You're in Southfield. You're about 15 miles off."

* * *

...It is February, 2007, and you are in Daytona Beach for the 500. You have been coming here for seven years for the *Dallas Morning News* and now you are also here as part of ESPN's *NASCAR Now* crew. You stop at a liquor store on Atlantic Ave. to pick up some vodka to keep in the room. After all, you don't want to do all your drinking at the Ocean Deck or across the street from the hotel at the Oyster Pub.

You grab the vodka and a couple of mixers as the clerk at the cash register says, "Mr. Cowlishaw, good to see you back. Remember I told ya the 48 car was gonna win it all last year."

You nod. You wonder if the fact that you are a regular in this particular liquor store 1000 miles from Dallas constitutes a problem.

CHAPTER 8

THE FIVE PEOPLE YOU
WON'T MEET IN HEAVEN

"If you can't be with the one you love,
honey, love the one you're with."

—Stephen Stills

IN THE FALL of 2002, when ESPN came calling, I was willing to listen. That was about it really.

More money? Sounds great.

Regular gigs on TV? Not so good.

One of the things about being a sportswriter, you learn at an early age to despise your TV brethren in the profession. They are all about hairspray, perfect teeth, booming voices and, if they happen to get out of the studio to attend the occasional game, the ability to count backwards from three to one to begin their breathless reports.

As in "3-2-1—Their helmet logos were the only signs of STAR power shown by the Dallas Cowboys today as they were humbled by…"

(That's pretty good; remind me to send that to Ed Werder when we're done here).

Of course, you don't hear the 3-2-1 intro if you're sitting at home, throwing empty Coors cans past the big screen as TV reporters begin this sort of focused post-game reflection, but I think you get the picture.

Ted Baxter as TV anchorman 30 years ago on *The Mary Tyler Moore Show* is a shining example of the print media's collective opinion of what they have always regarded as their more pampered but less informed colleagues.

Besides, my occasional appearances in local TV studios had generated no Emmy nominations. Two years of regular appearances on Jimmy Johnson's local show in '92 and '93 had given me excellent access to the Cowboys head coach, not to mention dozens of free beers at On the Border where we watched ESPN's Thursday night college games after taping.

But beyond that, I wasn't entirely certain that sitting in front of a camera was ever going to be in the cards for me, and I was fine with it.

It was no different really in 1998 when I first got the call from *Morning News* sports editor Dave Smith to replace Randy Galloway as the section's lead columnist (a move that simultaneously upgraded both sports sections).

At the time, I was a 43-year-old hockey beat writer with five years on the Cowboys' beat and a couple of seasons following the San Francisco Giants on my resume.

I had always believed my versatility would be a considerable plus if a column opening ever presented itself. But not every sports editor was likely to see it my way, and, besides, these jobs tend to come available about once a decade so I wasn't holding my breath.

So my initial thought when Smith called to offer the column position was, "Shit, I've covered the Stars for three years, they made it to the Western Finals and just signed Brett Hull. I want to SEE what happens next."

But I'm not a total idiot. So, given the opportunity to latch onto the freedom that writing a column presents—combined with a $30,000 raise—I jumped on for the ride.

Besides, there is something to be said for being there to write columns off of all of a team's playoff games and skipping those February road trips to Minnesota and Edmonton.

Four years later, I was not necessarily looking to add to the work load. But a free trip to New York, two nights at the Essex House to discuss a new show that we were told was supposed to be something like *Pardon the Interruption* but also somehow quite different seemed like a no-brainer.

All I had been told on the phone was, to avoid the label of East Coast bias, columnists from each time zone were being asked to meet at the Carnegie Deli to discuss this new show. There was even talk that the show would be called *Time Zones.*

I had discovered that the other cities were Boston, Chicago, Denver and Los Angeles but was unaware which writers had been invited to the meeting.

I was hoping to run into my friend, Rick Telander, a columnist at the *Chicago Sun-Times*. Instead I bumped into his colleague, Jay Mariotti, in the elevator. First disappointment.

Already knew Jay, did not know him well. Wasn't altogether sure I wanted to change that.

An engaging young man (young by my standards, he was probably 35 at the time) introduced himself as "Bill Wolff the show's producer" as we crossed Seventh Ave. to get to the Carnegie. Before long, we were joined by T.J. Simers of the *Los Angeles Times*, Bob Ryan of the *Boston Globe* and Woody Paige of the *Denver Post*.

Even before Max Kellerman made his fashionably late appearance at the table, I remember thinking two things.

One was: Do I really belong here?

The other: Who are they kidding with this lineup?

I had known Simers since he was a beat writer covering the Chargers for the *LA Times* and I was covering the Cowboys. But all of them, including T.J., had been working at this column gig longer than I had and in some cases much longer.

All of them were, without question, more self-assured, less timid and considerably louder than me. And that was just while ordering lunch.

In the first hour at the table, I might have mumbled a few comments to T.J. while Bob, Jay, Woody and the youthful but incredibly full-of-himself Max traded opinions at increasingly higher decibel levels with "Can you even believe this other idiot?" looks on their faces.

Put it this way. Carnegie Deli is a famously crowded and noisy place at lunch where you can talk at full volume and not get noticed.

We got noticed. And not for the reasons we get noticed today after a decade of having our faces plastered on TV.

Only when the conversation somehow shifted to the Kennedy assassination, putting me both in my element and on my home turf, did I became a central figure of the discussion.

There's no point in relaying all of it here. You can read it in my next book: *Would the Absolute Morons Who Still Believe JKF Was Killed by Either Two Shooters or a Conspiracy Please Leave Those Of Us With a Clue Alone?*

I mean, Stephen King just wrote an 849-page book called *11-22-63* and he concluded the chances of Oswald having been the lone gunman "at 98 percent, maybe even 99."

If the conspiracy angle is a bit too fantastic for Stephen King's taste, I really think we need to move on.

Anyway, my vehemence on this subject was noted in such a way that when Nov. 22 arrived, about three weeks after *Around the Horn*'s premiere, we attempted to do a segment (roughly the equivalent of *Out of Bounds* in today's show) on the Kennedy assassination in which I could use my vast knowledge on the subject to dismiss my colleagues' conspiracy-fueled ignorance.

All I can tell you is that after two, maybe even three takes, we gave up and went on to something else.

But even if the JFK discussion at the Carnegie Deli began to convince me that I could hold my own with this group, that didn't address the second question, as in: Who are they kidding?

Do the producers know about the relationship, or I should say lack of one, between Paige and Mariotti? Do they even know that Woody fired him years ago in Denver? Are the producers sure that America is ready to cheer for Jay or Bob Ryan or T.J—or any of us?

I saw a roster filled with what many sports fans might quickly adopt as the villains of the show. No shortage of bad cops here. Where were the good guys?

On top of that—five white guys? All in our 40s or 50s except for the host? On ESPN? It didn't feel like this was something that anyone had entirely thought their way through.

My concerns began to diminish after we journeyed down to Greenwich Village for an afternoon of bowling and bonding at Bowlmor Lanes. Somewhere in the historical record it should be noted that the team of Cowlishaw, Simers and Kellerman had no trouble dusting off the likes of Ryan, Mariotti and Wolff.

Woody did not join us. He had gone to Yankee Stadium to cover Game 1 of the Yankees-Angels first-round series. To be frank, he was distant for much of the lunch, didn't seem interested in being part of the show and as he has said since, "I didn't think it would be on the air a month."

But as the pitchers of Brooklyn Lager were delivered and I displayed my bowling prowess, delivering games somewhere in the 150s-160s, I felt as much a part of this group—whatever it was to become—as anyone else.

Mariotti and his instant opinions on absolutely everything, Ryan and his encyclopedic knowledge of my favorite team, the Celtics, and even Kellerman's unmatched self-confidence— these things had lost their ability to intimidate as the beer began to flow.

In fact, Kellerman even coined a phrase for my ability to roll a second ball at a 5 pin or maybe a 4-7 and, confident that the ball was on track, turn my back to the pins and head back to the seats.

"I love the walkaway spare," he said.

But isn't a relaxed sense, even a heightened belief in one's own abilities generally the case after two or three or six beers? That's what makes Dan Jenkins' *10 Stages of Drunkenness* so perfect. He articulated what millions of sloppy-drunk sports fans have experienced so many times— going from "witty and charming" early in the evening, working your way through the "Fuck Dinner" and "Tease the Giants and the over" stages and eventually concluding with "Invisible" and "Bulletproof."

I remember we watched the Yankees-Angels game in a restaurant in the West Village that night, eating steaks and consuming more beverages. The next morning I knew the Yankees had won but for a million dollars, I could not have told you exactly how.

When Kellerman met the group at lunchtime wearing a Bernie Williams jersey, I surmised that the Yankees center-fielder had supplied his usual post-season heroics.

And while Wolff tried to apologize for doing or saying something offensive the previous night, his buddy, Kellerman, stopped him. "You weren't even the drunkest one there," he said before casting a finger my direction.

Oh, well. Not an ideal start to a new relationship.

But, for me, not exactly something unexpected, either.

* * *

For unknown reasons, ESPN doesn't like us to talk about rehearsals for the show. So I won't dwell on the fact that I spent 16 days in October, 2002, anywhere from one to four hours at a time, seated in front of a camera on a small set ESPN had built on the third floor of the *Dallas Morning News* building, practicing for the show.

Once we made our debut in November, the critics who write about TV coverage in sports sections were close to universal in their disdain for the show. *USA Today*'s Rudy Martzke, who had made himself a must-read in the TV industry with some of the lamest Monday morning staples one could imagine, hated the format and said Kellerman's screaming "insults the ears."

Max, of course, loved that since it's such an awkward phrase. Without saying, "My, what big ears you have," how exactly does one insult a viewer's ears?

Assault? Maybe.

But the concept of writers scoring points or losing them as they shouted over each other to be heard—well, let's just say it was new and not exactly a fully formed concept when it hit the air.

And while *PTI*'s Tony Kornheiser and Michael Wilbon featured two widely respected columnists from the

Washington Post, there were plenty of sportswriters or columnists around the country who held our show's regulars in a lower level of regard.

Woody, in particular, seemed to be doing his own show. I wasn't the only one that complained to Wolff that he was impossible to follow. Going after Ryan or Mariotti and disagreeing with them was challenging enough for me and my self-doubts.

Trying to pick up where Paige had left off in his one-man comedy routine was impossible.

In addition, I thought we were all being limited in what we could provide the viewers by Paige and Mariotti going back and forth at each other every day. They were the only "panelists" that appeared every day unless forced to travel for their newspapers. And Mariotti displayed a remarkable ability to be in one city covering a World Series one night and back in Chicago the next day at noon to tape the show.

While Woody and Jay did five shows a week, the rest of us, soon to be joined by Michael Holley in Boston and Bill Plaschke in Los Angeles, were picking up two or three shows a week.

But Wolff and the other producers had made two decisions right from the outset. One was that Woody was going to be the star of the show, even if some days that meant little more than being the butt of Kellerman's jokes. The other was that the Paige-Mariotti rivalry, however rooted in reality it might be, was going to be the constant that would make or break the show.

For seven years, as the show grew and matured and got—I am proud to say—immensely better, I would still get asked if

Woody and Jay really didn't like each other or if they were just yelling at each other because they know it makes good TV.

I tried to remain consistent and honest in my response by saying, "Yes and yes."

* * *

I can't sit here today and tell you that I do a great job on the show. I can say without any hesitation that in that first year, I was terrible.

It took months, especially when I was getting a lot of one-show weeks, to become comfortable with even raising my voice, much less approaching Paige's decibel level, with news reporters, seated all around me.

One thing the producers didn't consider—no one could have possibly considered it in hindsight—was that news-rooms would be such depressing places in 2003 and 2004. People weren't reading papers, advertisers were fleeing, Craigslist was turning the classified ad goldmines into ghost towns—these things led first to buyouts and then to mass terminations all around the country.

The *Dallas Morning News* was not exempt.

Those fortunate enough to remain in the newsroom weren't always in the best frame of mind. And here I was with my little studio having been built in the middle of the room so I could talk about Britney Spears and J-Lo in "The Lightning Round."

I never heard a truly discouraging word from any of the reporters trying to work the phones and do real newspaper work while I learned to block out all that was around me and shout my opinions at the camera lens facing me.

Actually, it was years into the show when a female re-porter, riding the elevator down after taping one day, said, "I don't get why you have to be so loud."

I told her I was considered the quiet one on the show.

She shook her head in disbelief as she got off the elevator.

* * *

While *Around the Horn* began to collect far better ratings than the 5 p.m. Eastern shows that had preceded it, I gradually figured out what the show was about and how I could be-come a useful part of it.

During that first meeting back at the Carnegie Deli, Wolff had asked everyone at the table to name their favorite sporting events. I guess he didn't know that jaded sports col-umnists don't have things like favorite sports. They mostly have deadlines they try to meet in a semi-satisfying way.

But the guys were mostly polite and talked about Super Bowls and Final Fours of recent memory. When Wolff got to me, I said, "The Stanley Cup playoffs and the Daytona 500."

In its own way, my role on the show was created at that moment as Wolff talked about how much love he had for both.

Now that did not mean the show would have a lot of love for NASCAR or hockey, especially in the early years. When it came to hockey, the producers were mostly a slave to the ratings gods. As I would argue for more hockey during our conference calls, they remained steadfast in their opposition. "No one's watching hockey, so we're not talking about it," they would say.

When I would mention how NASCAR's ratings regularly buried things like baseball or college basketball, their response was more along the lines of: "No one here understands it, so we're not talking about it."

Through the years, I have to say the NHL has made more inroads to the show than NASCAR.

One other thing Wolff told us that first day in New York City was that if anyone said our show was like *The Sports Reporters*, the long running and successful Sunday morning show taped in New York, he had failed miserably.

Wolff, who left initially to go to Fox with Kellerman and has since been successful in producing MSNBC's prime-time programs including the *Rachel Maddow Show*, did not fail.

The two shows are nothing alike. And while I certainly respect Ryan, the only columnist who appears on both (I made one brief and not altogether memorable appearance on *Sports Reporters* in 2001), I think the average sports fan would rather see one of the *Horn* regulars show up at the barstool beside him than one of the Sunday morning regulars.

At the very least, our group wouldn't have to stand on those stools to see over the bar.

For years, I did not hesitate to check out pubs across the country to make sure I was correct about this.

Mitch Albom may have me by a few million in book sales. But I guarantee I've got him beat by hundreds of free shots.

* * *

The biggest change to the show came on Super Bowl weekend in 2004 when we learned that Kellerman and Wolff were leaving to go to Fox. Woody had been involved in the talks for some time as well, but he got a much bigger deal than the rest of us had with ESPN to move to New York and do our show as well as *Cold Pizza* from there.

Tony Reali got the official call at home sometime during the Patriots-Panthers game, something along the lines of, "Oh, Max is gone, and you're hosting the show tomorrow, find a nice suit to wear and good luck."

I don't know that anyone at ESPN saw him as a permanent answer—he was considered the "interim host" for months—but as it turned out, nothing did more to improve the show than Reali's arrival.

I don't say that with any disrespect towards Max. I liked him from the start and I believe he's a borderline genius (at least I think that's what he told me those seven years he spent at Columbia were for).

But I'm not sure his smart ass from New York angle worked as host. So they got someone who's slightly less of a smart ass from New York in Reali. And they found someone who initially made the show more about the panelists and less about the host's attitude, even though through the years Reali's guidance of the show has become so complete that when he takes a week off every two or three years, the show pretty much falls apart.

* * *

On our show, mostly we discuss wins and losses. Heroes and goats. Games that turn into upsets, quotes that make you laugh, gutless performances that make you want to cry. It's the usual sports fare that gets discussed around water coolers, on playgrounds and in bars across the country. That's the whole idea.

But, the 21st century being what it is, we also talk about players in trouble with the law. Maurice Clarett, Plaxico Burress, Michael Vick, Gilbert Arenas—the outlaw roll call is a lengthy one.

It was during spring training of 2008 that we were discussing what should be done about Cardinals Manager Tony La Russa, who had been charged with Driving Under the Influence after he apparently passed out in the driver's seat of his car after a night of too much wine.

It wasn't the easiest thing for me to discuss.

Between the hour-long conference call to prepare for each show and the 90 minutes to two hours it takes to tape, I spend more time with my colleagues than I do with any friends. But sometimes you don't even share your darkest secrets with your closest friends.

And in the spring of 2008 no one connected to *Around the Horn* knew what had happened to me in the summer of 2007.

CHAPTER 9

HANDCUFFS

"Here's to waking up at night
Half-drunk in a ditch by the side of the road
You're still thinking that you can't go on like this
Headed for a break down."

—*Before I Break* by Uncle Tupelo

IT WAS 3:16 A.M. on July 21, 2007—too damn early to have to be up on a Saturday or just way too late to be driving on a Friday in Caddo Mills, Texas, depending upon one's point of view—when James Ammons of the Hunt County Sheriff's Department flipped the switch on his overhead lights.

The Toyota Highlander in front of him was not speeding. It was not weaving. It wasn't doing anything out of the ordinary other than driving on the wrong side of the road.

Of course, if you're accustomed to driving in Dallas, two-lane frontage roads along highways are one way. In Hunt County, just across the Dallas County line, they are two-way roads.

"Why you driving on the wrong side of the road?" Ammons asks in a friendly tone as he approaches the driver's window. The response of the driver, already handing the officer his license and registration, is inaudible.

Ammons: "Where you headed to tonight?"

Driver: "I'm going home."

Ammons: "Where you live at?"

Driver: "Coppell."

Ammons: "You know where you're at?"

Driver: "Yeah."

Ammons: "Where?"

Driver: "Uh. Not in Coppell."

Ammons asks the driver to step out of the vehicle and that's when I make my debut in what may one day find its way into the archives of "World's Most Boring Police Videos."

It's not my best work. And if you've ever seen *Around the Horn* when we are forced to talk European Premier League soccer, you know that's saying something.

I own what I believe to be the only copy of this video. My lawyer Keith, who strongly advises me not to mention the video to anyone, thinks another one might be floating around in the Hunt County Sheriff's Department. But he is not sure.

All I can say to anyone whose time management is so poor that they locate a copy is that I hope to God you're an insomniac. You're sure as hell not going to make any money out of it.

It was more than two years after this incident before I ever watched it. Certainly I didn't want to see any part of it while I was still drinking on a nightly basis. And my lawyer's review of the tape, just days after my incarceration, had not been encouraging.

"I've seen worse," he said. "But I've seen a lot better. You were fucked up."

* * *

At 3:18 a.m., Ammons asks me to follow the light of his pen with my eyes without turning my head. For three minutes, I do this reasonably well although Ammons catches me cheating near the end. "Follow it all the way," he says.

Well, shit, if you do that, you have to turn your eyes so far they will fall out of your head, but whatever.

Next comes the heel-to-toe drill.

If there were any questions up to this point as to where this wee-small-hours-of-the-morning encounter was headed, it ends right here. I may have bluffed my way through the "follow with your eyes" portion of the exam.

Once we get into walking a straight line, connecting heel to toe for nine steps, turning and then walking back towards my car, arms to be at my sides the entire time, well—just rename the video *Sportswriter on Wire.*

It may be a semi-flat frontage road but the way my arms are flailing, I might as well be Philippe Fucking Petit tight roping from one World Trade Center tower to the other.

The highlight of this segment is Ammons walking beside me and dictating into his microphone in an east Texas twang that conjures images of Slim Pickens in *Dr. Strangelove.*

"Missed heel to toe, missed heel to toe, missed heel to toe, improper turn, missed heel to toe, missed heel to toe."

Improper turn? What, I was supposed to signal or something?

By the third part of the test, you can see from the sag in my shoulders I have entered total give-up mode. Facing a ditch which at that point looks like a pretty comfortable place to go lie down and start life over again in the morning, I am supposed to extend either foot out in front of me six inches off the ground and count until Ammons tells me to stop.

OK, you know what? You go do this on a slight elevation facing downhill completely SOBER and see if your arms don't move from your sides or there isn't just the slightest wobble in your hips while keeping that foot steady.
Go ahead…

So how'd you do? Not that easy, is it?

Admittedly, I delivered more than a slight wobble as I waited for the test period to end so we could move on to something else like maybe reciting the alphabet backwards, an odd custom I have practiced for years and can do quite well even when slightly drunk.

Instead, the test is over. Strangely, when Ammons advises that he is placing me under arrest for suspicion of

Driving Under the Influence, my head snaps back. I am stunned to have failed the test.

If you were scoring my performance on a scale of 1 to 100, I might have earned about a 12. Yet somehow I thought I had a chance to skate on this whole thing.

At 3:27 a.m., my hands are cuffed behind my back as I look out over the empty fields of a small east-of-Dallas town called Caddo Mills. I'm wondering if my future isn't somewhere behind me in those cuffs as well.

An arrest on my record—figuring out how to post bond—getting my car back—finding a lawyer—keeping this out of the *Dallas Morning News*, not to mention the hallowed halls of Bristol, CT where I was just a few months into a 2-year contract with ESPN's *NASCAR Now* on top of my regular job on *Around the Horn*...

There was a lot to consider at this very moment.

And so after pondering all of this while the officer got my money out of my car and waited for the tow truck to arrive, what's the first thing I asked him when he got into the car to drive me to jail?

"I have a question," I said. "These are not your priorities, I know. How do I expedite this situation so I can play golf in the morning? I have an early tee time."

Unexpected use of the word "expedite" raises my drunk test score to 14, but understand that by now it is 3:50 a.m. We are miles away from the jail. When we arrive, there will be finger-printing, an interview and a fair amount of standing around before I even see the jail cell. In the morning—remember it's a Saturday—I'm going to have to wait for the judge to arrive, then be hauled in front of him to hear the charges and enter a plea, then call a bail bondsman, wait for him to arrive at the jail to get me out, find someone else to give me a ride to my car in Royse City, pay to get it back, figure out exactly where the fuck in east Texas I am...

And I am wondering if I still have a shot at a 9 a.m. tee time in Dallas.

You gotta love the single-minded purpose of the dedicated golfer.

* * *

Before we continue the Tim-bashing segment of this chapter, let me speak on my behalf for a moment. Caddo Mills is 34 miles from downtown Dallas. I left the Corner Bar just off North Central Expressway and McCommas, about 2 miles north of downtown, before 2 a.m.

That's a long way to drive when you're drunk without hitting anything, without weaving, without bothering anyone. Kudos to me for that.

Now the fact that it's the ABSOLUTE WRONG DIRECTION TO BE GOING—well, I have to accept a points deduction for that.

My goal that night had to be to meet a few friends at the Porch on Henderson Ave., eat at the bar, have three or four beers (I guess that's the "three or four beers" I told the officer I had consumed) and drive home to get some rest before golf.

It was the *Dallas Morning News* annual sports department challenge. Writers vs. Editors. There will be blood. David Moore and I were set to kick some editing ass.

You ever have those nights that just get away from you though? You're convinced it's going to be a quiet night, a few beers or couple glasses of wine, then bed. Before you know it, you're standing next to a jukebox singing at the top of your lungs and telling a complete stranger you can't believe they have the audacity to close this fucking place at 2 a.m.!

If that's happened to you once or twice, well, try to avoid it in the future. It's not healthy for the liver, the wallet or anything else you can think of. If it happens to you a lot— stick with me for a few more chapters. You need to read this book as much as I need to write it.

* * *

It was nearly 5 a.m. by the time I was escorted down a winding Hunt County hallway behind the locked doors to the holding cell. With absolutely no buzz and only a thick tongue remaining from a drunken evening, this was becoming a slightly uncomfortable experience.

While I had not even begun to figure out how my evening had ended in east Texas, I had at least pondered what I figured to be the positives of the situation. Had I been hauled in on a Friday night in Dallas, the holding tank figured to be overcrowded. Wandering so far off course would at least give me my own cell for the night, I assumed.

Oops. Missed it by eight.

Actually, I was only the seventh to enter a 24 by 12 room with cement slabs projecting from the walls on each side and a toilet open to all with one roll of paper at the far end. But two more would join us before breakfast, so, I considered it a party of nine.

Slightly surprised to see three of my new roommates sleeping on the floor, I grabbed the last piece of slab available. Not that I slept. Mostly I laid there in a fetal position and thought about how much I didn't belong in this room.

There were people in here that looked like common criminals. Where the hell was the platinum level at this joint, anyway?

For the first two hours, there was no conversation. Snoring provided our limited soundtrack. And it occurred to me that all of us were sweating. The room was hotter than hell.

You have to understand something here. I like my hotel rooms cool. Some would say I like them cold. Beyond that, even if the temperature's ideal, there has to be a fan in place or some substantial sound emanating from the air conditioning vents. Otherwise sleep comes very slowly.

So, yeah, we had a whole list of hurdles to clear before I could even begin to contemplate the serious ones that I would face in the morning.

* * *

One question I have for the policymakers at the Hunt County facility—and maybe this happens elsewhere, I'm not a regular jailhouse resident so I'm not certain—but why did they have to take my CVS +150 reading glasses from me?

Was the risk that great that I would attack my fellow inmates with a tiny metal piece of the frame?

"Look out, boys; Cowlishaw's made himself a shiv. That motherfuckin' writer is crazy!"

Or was it a case of not wanting to be embarrassed when they found out I had dug my way out behind the toilet while my eight homies stood guard?

The reason I ask is that once morning came and the judge appeared and we all heard our charges and pled not guilty, an officer that had recognized me a few hours before told me I could call one of the bondsmen listed next to the phone on the jail wall.

He also asked me some Cowboys questions and said how much he enjoyed reading my columns in the *Morning News*. I thanked him as he left.

"You write for the paper?" asked one of my newfound friends.

I answered in the affirmative.

"Well, you need to write about this shithole," he said. A couple others perked up. Heads nodded.

"Tell people there's a nice air-conditioned room across the hall that sits empty just so they can throw all nine of us in here," he said.

I said I would be happy to if someone could help me with the phone since I couldn't read the names or numbers on the bail bond list.

The cellmate who had been identified by another as a registered sex offender during a conversation I did not carefully follow obliged.

It was 11 a.m. by the time I bonded out of jail.

The *Morning News* boys were making the turn by now, cursing my name and laughing about just how messed up I must have been the night before that I would lose my cell phone and couldn't answer their texts.

The editors repeated as champions of the sports department. I was held responsible.

There were problems of a much greater scale on the horizon, but to be honest, I thought a lot about how I had let my friends and co-workers down. It really pissed me off.

And I guess it was a lot easier than thinking about the shit I had really started the night before.

* * *

It was a week before I met Keith Willeford, a Greenville attorney who had been recommended to me. He said he handled plenty of cases opposite the D.A. and felt confident that we could get the sentence reduced. But he didn't guarantee anything. And right off the bat he offered a warning that I should have already known but didn't.

"A DUI is a misdemeanor," he said, "but it really isn't any more. MADD has made it so it's a lot more than that. I would have an easier time getting you off if you had broken into your neighbor's house and gotten caught."

I told him I just wanted him to do the best he could and that I really only cared about two things.

"One is to get the charge reduced to something else since I don't have a record," I said. "The other is to keep this out of the papers. I can't handle any publicity."

Again, there were no guarantees. In fact, the chances of the latter didn't sound good at all.

"The D.A.'s a big Mavericks fan," Keith said. "Huge. He already knows you were in here last Friday night."

Well, crap. This was one instance where taking pictures or doing shots with someone who wanted to meet me just probably wasn't going to be enough.

* * *

There are some things most people know about driving while intoxicated from the television ads and the billboards. It's not as though the word hasn't leaked out in the last 10 years or so that drinking and driving will get you into some serious shit.

But I think there are lots of things people don't know as well. Certainly I didn't.

Did you know that in Texas if you refuse to take a breathalyzer test, you lose your driver's license for a longer period than if you fail one?

I didn't.

I had always heard not to take the test if you thought you were going to flunk. Well, I knew if I couldn't walk a straight line, I was way the hell past .08, so I declined the opportunity to take the test.

Boom. Six months without a license.

Now that's what happens to you AFTER your case is adjudicated. For the months leading up to that time, you don't have your license, either. You have a yellow piece of paper that says this is your temporary license given to you when you refused to take a sobriety test after being arrested for DUI.

Now that's not exactly the sort of information you want to share with the woman behind the Avis counter or the customers in line behind you every time you need to rent a car in Bristol, Tenn., or Darlington, S.C., or Los Angeles or Phoenix or anyplace else.

And so even before we got around to the part where I might lose my license for six months, I didn't have anything but that damned incriminating piece of paper for seven months.

I didn't need to rent cars that often while traveling for the *Morning News*. But to cover the races I was assigned to for *NASCAR Now* or to get from the Hartford airport to ESPN's Bristol headquarters 40 minutes away, I definitely needed cars.

Let's just say, in happy hindsight, it became an adventure. And the car rental counter was minor compared to another issue.

I had let my passport lapse in early 2007 because, frankly, I didn't have any overseas trips planned and didn't want to pay the fee. I hadn't really thought about the possibility of my driver's license being locked in a drawer in the Hunt County jail.

So for a 7-month period (that would soon turn into 13 months), I made two or three trips to DFW Airport every month without any form of identification other than an expired driver's license I had found in a nightstand at home.

I learned to truly envy those people who had the luxury of handing the TSA agent a driver's license. It almost seemed like they were cheating while, trip after trip after trip, I explained how I had just lost my license and, yes, I understood that I would have to go through the extra checking process.

(Surprising traveler's hint: It's generally faster to get through the metal detector lines at the Hartford-Springfield airport to tell them you don't have a license than to show them one. Seriously. At least this was true in 2008. Glad I could be here for you.)

* * *

After seven months of hiding the truth from almost everyone I knew, time had run out. Keith called and told me to come to the courthouse. He said he had cut a deal that most people would love but that I probably wouldn't.

I would not have to report to a probation officer.

I would not have to perform any hours of community service.

While still technically without a driver's license, I could get a permit that would allow me to drive for work at any hour both in Dallas and on the road.

All extremely good news.

But I would have to accept that I was guilty of a DWI. That was going on my record, and in addition to all the monetary consequences that come with it, I had to understand that a second DWI would produce real jail time.

It wasn't what I wanted but I realized that it was probably better than I deserved. I thanked my lawyer and told him not to worry at all about the second DWI. I didn't drink and drive any more. I had learned that lesson the hard way.

I didn't need to.

I no longer lived in Coppell. I had moved downtown. I had a place in Victory Park. Where the Mavericks play. Where the Stars play.

And where you can walk or take a $5 cab ride to all the best bars in Dallas.

Yep. I had learned a lesson all right.

CHAPTER 10

PASSING THE TEST,
JUST STARTING TO LEARN

"I strolled all alone through a fallout zone,
came out with my soul untouched."

—*Growin' Up*, Bruce Springsteen

IT WAS A weekend in August, 2008—the same one that Usain Bolt put it on cruise control at the 100-meter finish line to win Olympic Gold in—seconds—and despite his brief burst of athletic supremacy, I knew it was going to be a long weekend for me, even if I didn't see anything special coming out of it.

My six months' probation was just about over. By early September, I was going to regain that most precious possession for air travel—a valid driver's license. And while I never had to perform community service or report on a regular basis to a parole officer, I did have to complete a 12-hour education course that consisted of a Friday night,

Saturday morning and Sunday morning in a south Dallas classroom.

There were about 15 other first-time DWI offenders in the room. A man named Buz—with just one 'z' for some reason—was droning on and on about something. I sat in the next to last row, hoping just to blend in, avoid recognition and survive the 12 hours in order to get the credit I had to turn in to the insurance company.

I wasn't paying strict attention when Buz started having one "student" after another on the right side of the room—I was seated on the left—explain the circumstances that led to their arrest charges. People were opening up about their drinking problems, their illegal behavior behind the wheel, the depressing circumstances that led to their being in this rundown Redbird classroom on a Friday night.

And it suddenly hit me. I had to do more than just punch a clock in this room. I had to tell a bunch of strangers I would never see again my name (bad enough) and tell them my story (even worse).

So I did what came naturally. I lied.

Stating my name as William wasn't technically a lie. That is, in fact, my first name, although no one has called me that since the days of grade school teacher calling roll on the first day of class.

But I wasn't about to tell the sordid details of being more than 30 miles off course and driving the wrong way on a highway service road at 3 a.m. on a Saturday.

So I told a story about how I was playing golf and drinking a bunch of beer during the round because it was a hot day and how I was going to spend the night with a friend who lived near the course but he got called in to work on an emergency when we finished the round and suddenly I found myself having to drive back to Dallas.

I thought it was a ridiculous story made up on the spur of the moment, but several of my "classmates" nodded. They could see that happening. Hell, maybe it sounded like a good excuse.

Buz seemed to accept it just fine. Buz has been sober since 1979, and Buz runs a lot of these classes and Buz has seen and heard a lot worse.

Buz never got a DWI. He says he was hooked on alcohol and Vicodin for 15 years, and then quit. He gives his religious faith a lot of credit for his ability to stay sober, but he doesn't push religion on us.

He doesn't really play the "scared straight" card, either, which is good. Buz makes it clear he's on our side. He just wants us to watch these tapes that the law says we have to watch. He wants us to pass the test that the law says we must pass.

And he doesn't want to see us back here ever again. That would mean that we're next door taking a class from his boss, Mark. Mark had five DWIs by 1992. You could do that back in the day, and, yeah, the occasional repeat-repeat-repeat offenders still fall through the cracks, but it's a lot harder to avoid serious jail time if you're getting arrested for drunk driving one time after another.

Mark teaches the "recidivist" class. They have to log 16 weeks, not just 12 hours like us.

Before we get to the videotapes that will have us all laughing—the footage is so grainy and the acting so poor they kind of resemble '70s porn tapes but without the porn—

Buz gives us a questionnaire to fill out. It's confidential and it's not a test to be graded like the one we will have to pass Sunday morning.

This one has questions like:

Is someone close to you concerned about your drinking?

Do you believe your drinking may be causing you problems?

Do you feel like you are a normal drinker?

Do your friends or relatives think you are a normal drinker?

Have you ever awakened the morning after drinking the night before and found you could not remember a part of the evening?

Can you stop drinking without a struggle after one or two drinks?

Do you ever try to limit your drinking to certain times of the day or to certain places?

If I answered all of the above honestly in the summer of 2008, I would have said: Yes, yes, no, no, frequently, no, yes.

But I didn't. I lied on at least a couple because I was embarrassed. Besides, it was just a questionnaire, a time-filler to get through the 12-hour class.

On the second day of the class, Buz said he was going to call five "students" into his office to talk to them about their drinking. He said you didn't have to feel guilty about anything if your name was called; he just wanted to meet with us.

And, yes, in this class filled with lowlifes and losers (OK, I didn't actually call anyone that but I certainly wasn't out to add names to my Blackberry in the classroom), mine was the third name called.

I walked down the hall and sat across the desk from Buz. He asked me if I thought I had a problem, and I said, yeah, I drink too much a lot of nights because I feel a lot of pressure from work and from some failed relationships in my life.

Buz said the reason he called me down here was because I had answered "yes" to the question asking if someone was concerned about my drinking.

He asked who the someone was.

I said, well, it used to be my wife, but now it's my girl-friend. And we both chuckled a bit at that.

Buz asked me if I ever got the DTs. I said I didn't know what those were (knowing full well what they were).

He said they were Delirium Tremens, more commonly known to people as the "shakes" that some people get while going through alcohol withdrawal.

I wanted to say, "Yeah, actually Delirium Tremens is a beer they serve at the Idle Rich pub on McKinney but I pre-fer Stella." Instead, I told him that, yeah, I probably get a little uneasy at times but mostly I just have trouble sleeping if I haven't had a few drinks.

Buz gently suggested that I consider going to an AA meeting. I told him that my father goes to meetings and that I had thought about it and would consider it.

That was the end of the meeting. He wished me the best, and we walked back down the hall to the classroom. I was glad to have survived the meeting without being told I "had" to do anything. But Buz's good cop approach with no bad cop in the room was having a genuinely positive effect.

I wasn't interested in just surviving the 12 hours in the classroom. For the first time in maybe forever, I was starting to think about my life.

* * *

I became a more attentive student the rest of Saturday and then Sunday morning leading up to the quiz. Buz was practically serving us the material we would need to learn (or at least memorize) on a platter, but I was actually paying attention, anyway.

On Sunday morning, I scored 100. Take that, bitches. I'm a 4.0 student when it comes to DWI awareness classes.

Anything, ask me anything, go ahead…

The ability related to driving which tends to be first affected by alcohol or other drugs is: A. Judgment; B. Muscle control; C. Reaction time; D. all of the above.

Which of the following may be a defense against intoxication: A. Fatigue; B. Time; C. Drugs; D. Sweating?

The average alcohol elimination rate per hour is: A. 1 drink; B. .015 %; C. .05 %; D. .08 %.

A DWI conviction which includes a BAC of .16 or greater results in a three year driver's license surcharge of: A. $1,000 per year; B. $1,500 per year; C. $1,750 per year; D. $2,000 per year.

Which of the following (of those provided) is the best sign of alcoholism: A. Sleeping after drinking; B. Not having a job; C. Increased sexual ability; D. Drinking alone?

Your answers are A, B, B, B and D.

Don't worry if you missed one or two. The test isn't for you.

Is it?

CHAPTER 11

"MERRY CHRISTMAS, MR. COWLISHAW, YOU'RE IN CRITICAL CONDITION"

"So I'll meet you at the bottom
if there really is one
They always told me when you hit it you'll know it,
But I've been falling so long,
it's like gravity's gone and I'm just floating."

—*Gravity's Gone*, Drive-By Truckers

THE OSCAR MADISONS had left the press boxes by the time that I got into the sportswriting game. Most of them were gone, anyway. That's not to say that there weren't any hard drinkers in the newsroom. That's not to say there aren't a few even now, hiding their hangovers in cubicles as they stare at blurry computer screens.

But they are the exception to the rule that provided the prevailing view of the newsroom going back to 1930s cinema and right up through Pete Hamill's marvelous *A Drinking Life*.

When I joined a mostly young *Dallas Morning News* staff in 1983—in the midst of what will one day be viewed as the last great era for newspapers and for sports sections in this country—sure some of us went out for beers after work. A couple of us might have been easily recognized as the ones most likely to be over served.

I have to admit that as much as I wanted to get from Oklahoma City to Dallas in 1983 to cover professional teams and move my career on down the tracks, the opportunity to drink beer after Rangers games with columnist Randy Galloway was near the top of my wish list.

And when a little more than a year into my *Morning News* days, I found myself in some rundown Detroit bar outside Tiger Stadium, pounding post-deadline beers with Mr. Randy after the '84 World Series—my God, life was good.

But most of the time, even on the good nights, the nights where you felt like you were part of that drinks-after-deadline scene you had watched in so many movies, it felt like you were just playing a role in one of them. An impostor.

Heck, you couldn't even stick a press pass in your hat to look the part because none of us had those cool hats.

* * *

If an era was dying in the mid-80s, so was Joe Miller, the owner of the bar on Lemmon Ave., where you would have been most likely to find a handful of reporters from the *Dallas Morning News* or the *Dallas Times Herald* talking with local lawyers, cops and judges.

In the spring of 1985, I met a part-time bartender there named Lori Winger, second cousin to Debra Winger and future wife and mother of my two children. We went to Joe's memorial service in 1986. We married in 1987, had Rachel in 1991, Ben in 1995.

By 2004, we had separated. It would be disingenuous to say my drinking played no part in it. Any other details of what may or may not have led to separation and, years later, divorce are irrelevant to the story being told here.

I do want to say this.

If you have ever had a failed relationship with a wife or girlfriend or husband in which your drinking was an issue, you may or may not have a problem. I'm certainly not qualified to judge.

If you have had two or more failed relationships in which your drinking was in issue, then you don't even need to think about it. You need to put this book down for five minutes and write down a list of those exes who thought you had a problem.

Next to each name, write down why you think they were wrong and how you know that you don't have a real drinking problem.

And good luck with that.

Lori wasn't the first to raise my drinking as an issue, and even though we would be together for two decades and produce two wonderful kids, she was not the last.

* * *

It may seem odd that even as an important relationship that had begun there dissolved and with Joe himself having been felled by cancer years ago, the modest building that had been Joe Miller's continued to play a part in my life. When I say "modest," that might be the biggest understatement in this book. If you don't know the Loon is tucked in at the end of that strip that has a cleaners, a Qdoba and a State Farm office, you will never find it.

By 2000, it had become The Loon, still nothing to look at from the outside (there isn't a single window in the place nor anything as trendy as "patio seating"), popular not just for offering any food at all (which Joe's didn't) but some of the best bar food in town in an area that quite frankly has a lot of good bar food.

The Loon is known for several other things. One of them is rude bartenders, a portrayal that might have been true a few years ago but was inaccurate the last time I checked. Another is that they serve some of the strongest cocktails in town, a concept that began back when it was Joe's.

Highly Accurate.

A third is that The Loon is open 365 days a year. Lots of people in Dallas, many of the young professionals that live in the Uptown area, aren't from here. On holiday nights when others might be inclined to stay home with family, they have none. It's not unusual to see a line out the door at 10 p.m. on Thanksgiving. I know. I've been in it before.

Dec. 25, 2008, was like most any other Christmas days of the last few years. My parents live in north Dallas. My brother and his family live in Dallas as well, at least when his kids aren't off at OU, studying and pretending it's a viable college on the same level as UT (what are they thinking with that?).

Lots of presents, lots of food, lots of games. By about 8 p.m. or so, everyone wears down and retreats to their respective houses.

About 9 p.m., I was settling into my couch, vodka-and-soda in hand since my driving for the day was over. A friend in town from Austin sent a text message saying he and his brother were going to The Loon to watch the Mavericks-Blazers game in Portland.

I was tired, but there wasn't a lot of arm-twisting needed. A $5 cab from the W to The Loon, two or three cocktails there, another $5 cab home—a chance to see a good friend and a relaxing way to finish a nice holiday with no work tomorrow.

What could possibly go wrong?

* * *

At 1:16 a.m., the ambulance picked me up somewhere near my apartment downtown. The admitting diagnosis at Parkland Hospital reads:

1. Alcohol intoxication.
2. Asthma.
3. Temporal contusion and temporal tip subdural hemorrhage.
4. Right parietal scalp laceration approximately 4 cm in length.

* * *

I have a vague recollection of talking to two men as they stopped the bleeding from the right side of the back of my head. Actually, one of them might have been a woman, I'm not sure. Their names aren't on the report. I do recall riding a short distance in the ambulance.

And yet I have no memory of either cab ride to The Loon and only the vaguest memories of watching a few minutes of the Mavs game there with my friends. I spoke to a young woman named Kallie for a short time. Without a doubt I had at least three or four vodka sodas there, drank them quickly and left on my own, as was my habit. My friends say I was there for a while and then, all of a sudden, I wasn't.

I still can't tell you exactly where I fell and cracked my head open. The address on my records from Parkland is my building, so I'm guessing I fell just outside on the sidewalk. There is nothing in my records that says who called 911, so it's possible I managed it myself.

All I know is that at some point in the wee small hours of Dec. 26, 2008, I was lying awake in an emergency room thinking, "Well, I'm not the most famous person to come to Parkland with an open wound to the right side of my head."

* * *

The Parkland report continues:

1:51 a.m. Pt (patient) arrives after falling over and hitting his head on a corner. Pt arrives slurring words and smells of ETOH. PT lac bleeding, not well controlled with either direct pressure or pressure bandage. MD aware. Pt placed in room 28 for lighting and eval problems.

2:37 a.m. PT has soaked through 2 pressure bandages and 10 packs of 4X4s. MD attempted to place staples, but bleeding to lower portion of cut shoots blood approx 8 cm away from head. Pressure being held by RN without slowing or cessation of bleeding. Surgicell X 2 placed to head with additional pressure held X 5 minutes and cessation of bleeding. Pressure wrap placed with ice pack over lac, will check site in 15 minutes to monitor for additional bleeding. Pt to go to CT scan.

3:23 a.m. Pt back from CT. Ccollar/spinal precautions in place.

4:46 a.m. Morphine 4 mg ivp given.

4:57 a.m. Dr. G at bedside, removed staples on patients right parietal area and washed out head laceration. Two arterial bleeding vessel sutured by Dr. G. Patient tolerated the procedure well.

* * *

This all comes from the official report. I remember little of this. Really hadn't expected to do any morphine on this particular night.

I do know that at some point early in the morning I began to tell the nurses that came in and out of my view that I needed to leave soon because I had a flight to Philadelphia the next day for the Cowboys-Eagles game on the 28th.

That mostly drew laughs except for one nurse, who shouted, "You're in critical condition. You're not going anywhere."

Now I have about 200 pages of paperwork and don't see a mention of critical condition anywhere. I also didn't see it in writing that I arrived with a .26 blood alcohol level but my friend, Dr. Mickey, found it for me.

That should be about 13 drinks, but given the manner in which The Loon loads them up, not to mention me pouring a couple for myself before going to the bar, I'm going to say seven or eight could have gotten me to that stage.

* * *

We live in an age in which we don't have to rely upon medical records for information on hospital stays. We can go straight to the most random of blog sites and, if you have achieved even the modest degree of fame that comes from ESPN appearances—voila.

There you are.

* * *

Excerpt from a blog post following the incident:

I hinted at this in my early picks post, and before I reveal the story, just a few caveats. I have absolutely nothing against Cowlishaw. I have not read a single one of his columns, but I do think he is one of the few tolerable people on the terrible show, Around the Horn. A friend of mine told me about this on New Year's Eve, but I waited for all the details before I posted it.

The facts: on December 26th Tim Cowlishaw was admitted to a Dallas emergency room with a head wound.

The story: The day after Christmas, Tim Cowlishaw got out of his mind drunk, partied way too hard, fell down, and busted his head open.

The funny part: He passed out in the hospital that night due to being completely wasted, head busted, and pain medicated. He woke up the next day, December 27th, and started freaking out and screaming, "I have to get to Philadelphia, I have to get to Philadelphia!!!" (The Cowboys were playing the Eagles with the playoffs on the line). He tried to leave the hospital but the doctors wouldn't let him.

The things I found hardest to believe about the story: Cowlishaw is 53. I figured he was 45 at the oldest. I'm not good at judging age, but Cowlishaw looks pretty good for 53. Then again, the only time I see him he is next to Woody Paige, Bob Ryan, and Bill Plaschke, so I guess it is easy to look young.

Also, Cowlishaw was with an absolutely smoking hot chick. I figured he was famous around Dallas, but I was a little shocked to find out how hot this chick was. I was told he has absolutely no problem getting seriously hot tail in Dallas. Sort of amazing.

The Proof: Unfortunately, other than my track record of being a completely honest and standup guy, I don't have much proof. It was one of my really good friends that was the eye witness, not me.

Also:
There was nothing posted on Cowlishaw's Blog between Dec 22 and Jan 1. *Tim Cowlishaw Blog.* And, Cowlishaw had no columns between Dec 24 and Jan 4. Tim Cowlishaw *Dallas News*

Of course it was the holiday season, so it's easy to understand why he didn't write anything. But then again, you think he would have written *something* for the Dallas/Philly game, right?

* * *

I think seeing this story on the Internet a week after I had been released from the hospital bothered me nearly as much as the experience itself. It shouldn't be that way, so make of that what you will. It bothered my doctors at Parkland to learn that someone in their emergency room felt it was their place to pass along emergency room information.

It's not entirely accurate. It's off by a day, and I did not attempt to leave the hospital on my own although as I mentioned, I wanted to. I wasn't even allowed out of bed the first 24 hours.

Yes, my girlfriend Megan did arrive in the early morning hours after I managed to get a text message to her about what had happened. I'm not going to dispute the blogger's description of her. If he's a bit misguided in general about my having "no problem getting serious hot tail," well, who am I to correct every blog in town?

And as for this part about *Around the Horn* being awful, hey, what's up with that?

Actually, this blog wasn't seen by many people and received only a few comments over the next few months.

But it may have done as much to make me realize the need to curb my drinking habits as anything else that happened that Christmas weekend.

Even a year after the incident, if you Googled my name, "Tim Cowlishaw drunk" this story would pop up in the No. 5 or 6 spot.

Knowing that your kids' friends have such ready access to this information is, in fact, sobering.

So to whoever's blog this is: Your reporting is a little shoddy and your Parkland friend is an asshole.

But thanks.

* * *

On Dec. 28, I watched the Eagles destroy the Cowboys 44-6 from my private room at Parkland. I had graduated from the emergency room the day before.

The Cowboys weren't going to the playoffs. Tony Romo said that if this was the worst thing that ever happened to him, he figured he'd lived a pretty good life.

I felt the same way when I was released that Monday. My head didn't hurt but it felt really awkward with all those staples and stitches back there. And I was instructed not to drive for at least a few weeks, a figure I quickly reduced to a few days.

Memories of seeing my kids and my 82-year-old father visiting me in the hospital hurt the most. I never wanted my dad to go through something like that again. We're supposed to comfort our parents in hospitals, not the other way around.

As for my kids, my daughter was five months away from graduating high school. My son was five months away from finishing middle school. Little did I know I was just five months away from my next weekend in a hospital.

The notion that I might not be there to provide for them because I had bled to death on the Houston St. sidewalk outside my apartment on Christmas night with an alcohol level of .26…

How could that be me? I was successful, I worked two jobs, I was the guy in the paper and the guy on TV. How could I still find a way to be that irresponsible on a moment's notice when a friend called to meet for a drink—at age 53?

It wasn't the kind of thing I could bring myself to spend too much time pondering.

So I didn't.

Just before I was released, I was given a reading and writing test to make sure my brain was functioning properly. I was also given what I might call an education seminar on what can happen to people that suffer major head wounds.

Some of the final notes from Parkland:

Pt sitting up in chair, talking on cell phone. Pt agreeable to evaluation though easily irritable at explanation of stroke. Pt anxious, eager to go home. Pt alert and attentive to all tasks. Don't expect focal language deficit. Pt has coherent sentence formation.

I like that last line—coherent sentence formation suddenly not a problem. Good news at last for *Dallas Morning News* readers.

* * *

One more thing that I don't remember but I have been told and I have no reason to think it's anything other than true: On the night I had come home to my apartment, about eight hours after being released from Parkland hospital, I asked Megan if she thought it would hurt if I had one drink. Just to relax a bit. After all, I hadn't taken any of the hydrocodone that had been prescribed for me.

She got very angry. She said no, it wouldn't be OK at all.

I didn't get mad. She did and went to bed.

Then I had that drink.

CHAPTER 12

A NEW RADIO SHOW AND
A SEIZURE TO GO WITH IT

"When we're deeply in love with drink, we have no idea
what kind of fire we're playing with."

Drinking: A Love Story by Caroline Knapp

MY FIRST MEMORIES of record albums were those
that belonged to my parents when we lived in New Jersey.
These were primarily the popular soundtracks—*My Fair Lady*,
South Pacific, *West Side Story*—of the early '60s.

The fact that I could walk around our New Jersey streets
at age 8 singing, "There is nothing like a dame…" or "I've
Grown Accustomed to Her Face" without being either
scarred for life or, more important, physically scarred by
other kids tells you we lived in a pretty safe neighborhood.

My parents also had a comedy album that troubled me
greatly. It was Jackie Mason's *I Am the Greatest Comedian In the
World—Only Nobody Knows It Yet*.

As a second grader with no sense of irony, this bothered me to no end. In my mind, Red Skelton was the funniest man on television. I had never even seen this Jackie Mason. And yet here was proof—I thought—that he was, in fact, the greatest comedian on the planet.

(It wasn't until nearly 40 years later, seeing Jackie Mason's one-man show on Broadway that I realized he wasn't far from the truth).

This is just my way of offering a brief introduction to *Threewide—The Greatest Sports Talk Show in the History of Dallas Radio.*

It was in the fall of 2008 that I got a call from a new radio sports talk station in Dallas. The whole thing ended badly for me and the good people I worked with a few months later, so let's just call this station, oh, how about 105.3 The Fan, Dallas' local CBS affiliate.

Just to give it a name.

Anyway, despite the fact that I had a full-time job as columnist for the *Dallas Morning News* and a part-time job doing *Around the Horn* that tends to take up a considerable number of hours a week, I thought maybe I could squeeze in another two hours a day doing drive time radio five days a week.

The good folks (initially) at The Fan thought so, too. Ben Rogers and Jeff "Skin" Wade already had a show at the station. It was somewhere in between sports talk and guy talk. They had been working together only since about the third grade as best friends growing up, strangely, in Richardson, Texas as well.

What are the odds of three guys from Richardson working together 20 years after high school (OK 20 for them, more like 35 for me) at a big-time Dallas radio station?

Well, the odds are against it and we didn't quite make it. This wasn't big-time. Not in facilities. Not in the people running it. And not in, sadly, our ratings which seemed to reflect that 99 percent of the local radio listeners had not caught on to the fact that this really was *The Greatest Sports Talk Show in Dallas History*.

It started off just fun as hell to be honest with you. Ben and Skin made fun of me for my big, obtuse sports brain. I made fun of them for never having covered sports and not really knowing shit about anything other than Skin's almost scary understanding of the most arcane aspects of the NBA's salary cap.

But we had fun, and if no one was listening, well, too bad. We had the Rangers' Michael Young on for 15 minutes one day without one mention of baseball. Young's a big movie-goer who has seen everything so when we got our 64-movie bracket for "All Time Guys Movies" down to the quarterfinals, we had him on to give his opinions.

It was ridiculous stuff like *Usual Suspects* vs. *Caddyshack* and *Godfather II* vs. *Jaws* but Young was funnier and probably more insightful than he ever is when he's just fielding questions about the Rangers' playoff hopes.

Most of the time when we had guests, though, we had to do it in clandestine fashion. The guy who was entrusted with turning The Fan into the top-rated sports talk station in Dallas—there were two others firmly in place and killing it in the ratings—did not believe in guests.

Seriously. He had come up with what he believed was a foolproof formula that had worked in Philadelphia and Detroit and, by God, it was going to work in Dallas. Never mind the fact that those two cities and the general attitude of their sports fans are about as far removed from Dallas as Moscow.

Guests were bad. So we had to wait until, oh, did I forget to give him a name? Let's just call him Tom Bigby.

We had to wait until Mr. Bigby was out of town to have Larry Fitzgerald on when the Cardinals were heading into their first NFC Championship. Ever. We had to wait until Mr. Bigby was mending fences back in Detroit to have Charles Barkley on to talk Mavs and NBA playoffs.

It was crazy.

On top of that, all three of us were discouraged from giving our opinions. (I'm not making this up). We were instructed to get topics in play and then take call after call to hear what the listeners' opinions were.

Needless to say, we didn't do a very good job of playing by the rules or following the "Bigby Playbook" and this caused Ben and Skin a considerable level of concern. These were two guys with wives and two young kids each, and this radio show—they did 4 hours and I was just on for the final 2—was their sole source of income. And as the months crept along in the early part of 2009 and the ratings continued to reflect a general lack of enthusiasm for what we were doing, they knew from the one-sided contracts they had reluctantly signed that their days at The Fan were numbered.

For me, this was my third job and my smallest paycheck by far. But I won't go so far as to say I was doing it for fun. Having lost the NASCAR gig with ESPN at the end of 2008, my income had fallen by about 40 percent. With a daughter about to graduate from high school and head to the

University of Missouri, that out-of-state tuition I had rather inadequately prepared for was soon to become a reality.

So while I was no longer flying across the country to cover NASCAR races, I was writing four columns a week and doing two or three *Around the Horn*s a week and doing radio from 5 to 7 five days a week. There were aspects of this life that were exhilarating but they were also exhausting.

Shockingly, I chose to deal with them by drinking heavily.

OK, that's not a shock at this point. But despite Christmas holiday stay at Parkland Hospital, I had not cut back on my drinking at all. It was still two or three Coors Lights a night to get the ball rolling, then the shift to vodka.

This was in spite of the fact that Dr. Mickey had issued what was clearly a life-changing warning back in January of 2009—if only I had been listening. Dr. Mickey was the neurologist who checked on my condition two weeks after my Parkland stay. He was also the man who removed all the staples and stitches from the rear of my scalp.

I'm not someone with an extraordinarily high tolerance for pain. I'm probably average at best. The removal of all of those stitches in the back of my head should have dispatched some sort of message to the undamaged portion of my brain that this whole drinking thing was going the wrong direction. But it didn't.

Neither did Mickey's message which was that there was a fairly high chance of me suffering a seizure in the next 9-to-12 months.

"A—what? Did you say seizure? What can I possibly do to avoid such a thing?"

Those were the questions an intelligent person might have asked. I never did. I just wanted to get the stitches out of my head and get the hell out of Mickey's office.

"There are two facts I tell people after they've suffered head injuries similar to yours," Mickey told me when I went back to meet with him for this book in the summer of 2011. "And I'm sure I told you these that day.

"The first is that the experience in World War II, in Korea and in Vietnam is that a soldier who has a penetrating brain injury—it can be from a bullet or a fragment, shrapnel or something—the solider has a 50 percent likelihood of developing seizures in a delayed fashion. The average time lapse between the brain injury and the first seizure is nine months," Mickey said.

"What most people think of a seizure is a 'grand mal' seizure. They think of someone biting their tongue, jerking their arms and all. That's just one type of seizure. A seizure is a short-circuiting of the normal electricity of the brain. The injury that you suffered made you a candidate for a temporal lobe seizure.

"The second fact that I would have told you is that there are three things that make the brain more likely to trigger a seizure. Those are sleep loss, hunger and alcohol. And those three tend to run together if you think about a typical scenario. Someone has six or eight or 10 drinks on a Friday night. They stay up very late. They don't get quality sleep. They skip meals the next morning. By the middle of the day, their brain is wired. A blow to the head sets the stage for this irritable seizure focus. This process can happen to soldiers. It can happen to people that fall off their bike.

"And it happened to you."

It happened to me on May 8, 2009. It could have been one of the highlights of *Threewide* or lowlights, depending upon one's point of view. But it happened near the end of the two-hour show and during a commercial break, so no one other than Ben and Skin and Troy Hughes, our board operator, was there to see or hear it.

I wasn't drinking at the time—I never drank on the show and I was never really much of a daytime or early evening drinker to begin with—but I had certainly been drinking a lot the night before and all that week. The previous night I had finished my drinking rounds at Kenichi, my usual final port of call since it's across the street from the building in which I live.

The manager and co-owner Josh Babb is my closest friend. We developed a bond when I got him free Radiohead tickets—great seats, too—shortly after he started at Kenichi in 2008. In return, I got free drinks.

Lots of free drinks. Many, many free drinks.

One day in 2010 I asked Josh before I stopped drinking how often he thought I was drunk when I left Kenichi.

"Ninety percent of the time," he said.

I told him there was no way. That was far too high. Josh shook his head.

"Ninety percent of the time you're drunk. Legally drunk. About 40 to 50 percent of the time you're wasted and I wonder if you will make it all the way home."

And, as I said, it's literally 40 yards from the door at Kenichi to the door of my apartment building across the street.

On the night of May 7, my final drink was the usual—
Stoli, soda, splash of cranberry. I think. There's no reason to
think it was anything different or more exotic. There's a
pretty good chance there was no vodka in the glass because I
was hammered.

"My bartenders knew at a certain point to just give you
soda with cranberry," Babb said. "You couldn't tell the
difference."

The next day I was my usual self at the radio station.
That is to say I was a bit on the shaky side, grabbing the
edges of the table in front of me at time for support. It was
nothing that anyone would notice but something I had grown
accustomed to doing. I didn't just do it at the station. When I
found myself in large clusters of reporters around an athlete
or, say, Jerry Jones after a Cowboys game, I had developed a
tendency to grab something or someone just lightly enough
that they wouldn't really feel it, but it would be enough to
keep me upright and avoid having the "shakes" take full
control.

OK, if you're getting the impression I was a bit of a mess
at this point, I'm with you. And, finally, late in the show on
May 8, during a break, I looked up at one of the TV monitors
in the room and felt like I just couldn't move any more.
That's the only thing I can really say to describe it. Mickey
says the kind of seizure I was having or was about to have
"tend to be very hard to describe later."

I felt like I had hit the wall and there was almost a per-
verse comfort in thinking I didn't need to move any longer.

Skin, standing just to my left, had been talking to Troy
when I heard him say, "Hey, man, are you OK?" But it

sounded like he was in a tunnel. I didn't respond. I hit the floor.

From what I am told, Troy rushed over to me and did what he could to make sure I didn't swallow my tongue. Troy was both an Eagle Scout and an Aggie and, frankly, I think he just wanted to develop a certain closeness to a former Longhorn, but, regardless, he was there for me. And I didn't swallow my tongue. I just shook a bit and fell to the floor.

The ambulance arrived at the radio station with astonishing quickness. They were there in less than 10 minutes from the time I fell. By then, I was sitting up on a couch in the office we all shared and while I wouldn't say I felt fine, I felt mostly OK. But I was going in and out of conversations and had a pretty loose grip on reality, so it was off to the hospital one more time. At least this time I was able to walk—with guidance to the ambulance.

* * *

University of Texas Southwestern Medical Center at Dallas
Hospital Encounter
Patient Name: Cowlishaw, Tim
Sex: Male
DOB: 3-31-1955
CHIEF COMPLAINT: Evaluation of new onset seizure
HISTORY: A 54-year-old male who was in his usual state of health until 05/08/2009 afternoon when he was at work and apparently does not remember feeling disoriented or confused himself; however, his father informs that he was talking about things that were not happening at the time. Information is obtained by review

of some of his medical records, interviewing him, and his father also provided some information. Per record, patient while working became unresponsive after a period of confusion, looking off to the side, and with "shaking movements." He did not bite his tongue. There was no bladder or bowel incontinence (*good to know*). He was subsequently confused for at least five minutes. Patient was seen by paramedics. According to patient, the whole episode may have lasted about 10 minutes. He has no previous history of seizure; however, his recent neurological history is remarkable for significant head trauma in December 2008 when he fell and hit his head against a corner of a table. He had mild right parietal depressed fracture associated with subarachnoid bleed and also a left anterior temporal contusion. Patient was admitted to Parkland on 12/26/2008 to 12/29/2008 and subsequently was followed by Dr. Mickey.

SOCIAL HISTORY: Nonsmoker. He uses 3-4 drinks of alcohol per night. Denies any history of drug abuse. Lives alone.

REVIEW OF SYSTEMS: No headaches, double or blurred vision. No difficulty with speech, swallowing. No chest pain, shortness of breath, any abdominal complaints. Bowel and bladder function is normal.

GENERAL: He is awake, alert and is oriented. Speech intelligible (*would they say that about Woody on a good day? Just a thought…*). Can follow commands.

IMPRESSION: New onset seizure activity, most likely post traumatic; however, his seizure threshold may have been lowered further by excessive alcohol usage and hyponatremia, sleep deprivation, etc.

RECOMMENDATIONS:

1. Patient needs to be treated for seizure disorder as it is likely to recur. Will start him on Keppra 500 mg

and increase dosage to 1000 mg twice a day subsequently.

2. Patient was advised that he should not drive for six months.
3. He would need outpatient follow-up for ongoing medication monitoring and treatment.
4. EEG is scheduled and is pending at this time.
5. Patient realizes that his alcohol intake has been excessive and plans to look into that. He was made aware of alcohol intake adverse effect on seizure control.

* * *

So there you have it. Am I a fast learner or what?

Give me a DUI, a blow to the head that has me bleeding all over the streets of Dallas on Christmas night and a seizure—and I'll put two and two and two together and come up with an answer.

Although physically I was in much better shape on this hospital visit than my previous one, mentally I was a wreck. Within an hour after being admitted and lying there in the emergency room, I was surrounded by my 82-year-old comforting father, my daughter three weeks shy of high school graduation, my 8th grade son who had endured some illnesses of his own that had caused him to miss most of the school year and would force him to attend summer school in a few weeks in order to move on to high school.

Ben and Skin were there, too, and between the three of us we were doing some of our best work with our usual absence of an audience. They kept the mood light. Heck, they were practically heroes to my son, Ben, who had never shown any interest in my newspaper columns and only occasionally (at that point) watched *Around the Horn* but listed to me with Ben and Skin almost every day.

Two things happened in the next two hours that would change my life. Forever (I hope).

After the usual amount of time, I was taken from emergency up to my own room. There was some preliminary talk about my condition, what they planned to do, the tests they wanted to give me over the next couple of days to make sure I as OK and not susceptible to another seizure right away.

In a moment that I can only compare to being handcuffed in the back seat of a Hunt County police car and telling the officer I really, really needed to make a 9 a.m. tee time the next morning, I told the doctor and nurses that stood at the foot of my bed I really, really needed to attend my daughter's end-of-the-year Lariette banquet the next night in Coppell.

I was willing to be driven there and then driven right back to the hospital if necessary. Rachel was giving a speech and there was just no way I was going to miss it. My travel for work had caused me to miss any number of dance recitals, track meets and other events although I am proud of my track record on that front. In 2006, as a sophomore, she performed at halftime of 11 Coppell games and I made it to all 11. It was only after the ESPN NASCAR gig had me travelling on so many weekends in '07 and '08 that I was forced to miss a handful of those games.

But now she was going to be all dressed up, giving a speech she was nervous about delivering in a hotel ballroom. I had to be there.

The doctor looked back and me and shook his head. I wasn't going to be there.

Rachel said it was fine. I knew it wasn't fine.

It was in this same period of time, as medical attendants came and went in my room that I was asked about my personal habits for the report you just read.

Do you take any kind of recreational drugs? "No."

Do you smoke? "No."

Do you drink alcohol? "Yes."

How much alcohol do you drink? "About three or four drinks a night."

Ben and Rachel stood a few feet away as I was being questioned. They wore blank expressions as I explained that I had a few drinks each night.

I think in their own ways they both knew I was being about as honest with the nurse as I was with myself. Who knows? Maybe they actually thought that I thought three or four was an accurate number. Maybe they thought it was just something you say to pass the test.

I don't know. I never spoke to them about that moment. It was too difficult. As good as I felt about many things I had done as a father, not just to provide for them but to be there for them whenever possible, I felt at that moment they were slipping away.

They weren't little kids. Ben had always been old for his age, and his bout with a blood disorder had matured him. He had been scared about his own mortality, an awful thing for a 14-year-old to endure.

Rachel was just 12 weeks away from getting the hell out of town and starting her new life at the University of Missouri.

She couldn't wait and for a lot of reasons. I was just providing her one more by allowing my drinking to send me back to the hospital and miss her one last big night of high school.

And that's when it happened.

That's when I knew my days and nights of drinking, of being the life of the party, had come to a crashing halt.

I didn't lay there and promise God I would be good. I didn't make any bargains along those lines. I'm not the religious type, much less one who invests any value in the power of prayer.

I just said: That's it. Get me outta here. I am going to stop, and people will be surprised that I'm going to do it my own fucking way.

CHAPTER 13

THE JOURNEY BEGINS

"Driver surprise me. Whatever works for you.
I'm brand new and reinvented.
Without a scratch, daisy fresh and arrow straight."

— *Driver Surprise Me* by the National

THIS WAS BEFORE I set out to stop drinking in 2009. In fact it was the fall of '06, the year before a DWI would serve as the first of my three "strikes" in the summer of '07.

I was in the fourth-floor office of Jim Moroney, publisher and CEO of the *Dallas Morning News*, which was strange enough because I had never before seen this office, much less been inside it. And to make matters worse, I was essentially arguing my irrelevance to the paper, telling him he could live without me much easier than he imagined.

Moroney, sitting on his couch instead of behind his desk to suggest "hey, we're all just pals here," took the opposite approach and went at it from an even more bizarre angle. He was telling me how important I was to the newspaper because his teenage son watched me every afternoon on *Around the Horn*.

It was almost as if the publisher of the newspaper where I had worked for 21 years was joining the chorus of Dallas-area bartenders who, on our initial meeting, tend to say things along the lines of: "Hey, Tim, good to meet you, I watch you on ESPN all the time. What are you doing in Dallas?"

So what prompted this bizarre meeting?

Throughout the spring and summer of 2006, I had talked with producers from ESPN about becoming part of their NASCAR coverage in 2007 when the cable giant's rights to the sport kicked in. I had flown to Bristol two or three times, met with different people, even auditioned as a possible host of *NASCAR Now* on one trip.

My immediate supervisors in the sports department at the *Morning News* were aware of all this as we were all under the assumption it would be for part-time work. But in the late summer of '06, two things happened to change the tone of these discussions.

ESPN began to show more interest in me devoting full-time work to NASCAR (while maintaining a presence on *Around the Horn*). And the *Morning News*, fighting the same losing battle for readers and advertising dollars as other newspapers across the land, was forced to offer buyouts for the first time.

I had no desire to stop writing or to leave the *News*. But as someone who had been at the paper more than 20 years, I was going to be offered a year's salary (50 weeks, technically) if I took the buyout.

ESPN was talking about a deal where I'd earn the same money as I made at the *News* (about $175,000), with the *Around the Horn* pay ($750 per show at that time) remaining a separate deal.

Suddenly, that one year's pay with no salary loss to follow as I changed jobs looked very intriguing. The chance to pay off credit card debt, put more money into college funds, maybe have a little fun money on top of that to get certain aspects of my life in order—I would stop short of saying it looked "too good to be true" but over time I decided, reluctantly, it was something that needed to be done.

I figured I could find some writing platform at ESPN, even if it was just NASCAR at first. No longer having a powerful voice in Dallas was troubling, but maybe being ahead of the curve on leaving the newspaper business was better than lagging behind it.

So I decided to take the buyout. There was only one problem.

It wasn't offered.

The *Morning News* designated a handful of employees as too valuable to lose. I was the only general columnist in sports, or on the news side, for that matter, to receive what I guess was meant to be a flattering note.

I went nuts—or as nuts as I ever go, which means I banged my fist into the filing cabinets in my office two or three times. Then I went to the sports editor and began working my way up the ladder to see who could do something about this injustice.

To be designated too valuable? Outrageous.

It's a difficult thing to go from one meeting to the next telling people, "Look, you're overrating me. Haven't you read my work? I'm not that good. Now let me go!"

And that's how at the end of this ladder climb I found myself seated across from Moroney, downplaying my significance to the product while he extolled my greatness.

Trying to soften the blow—of having to stay—Moroney mentioned that I was making a pretty good salary, even compared to anchors in local television which had been his background before coming to the *News*.

Then Moroney added this kicker.
"You know, you basically have a good job here, and you've practically got it for life—unless you develop too much of a fondness for Jim Beam or something," he said.

Mr. Beam was never a problem. Mr. Goose and his friends of the clear-colored liquor were increasingly becoming one, but Moroney had no way of knowing that at the time. The drinking gods would not shout "Strike One" at me until the following summer.

* * *

I kept this meeting with Moroney in my mind a lot in the first few days home from the hospital after my seizure in 2009. I wasn't sure I ever thought I came close to losing my job at the *Morning News* while spiraling downward those last three years since the meeting in the publisher's office.

Now I began to think Moroney—or more likely those bosses beneath him—could have started to have real concerns had I been just a little more careless or a bit more unlucky.

Sitting in the publisher's office and hearing the off-hand remark he made about Jim Beam without any knowledge of my drinking habits—well, I'd say a more God-fearing person would have taken that as a wake-up call or at least a sign that it was time to straighten up.

Instead, I had shrugged it off as if to hit a buzzer and say, "Ahhhh, wrong liquor, pal. Vodka not bourbon."

* * *

Ideally, this is where I would start typing in a diary of the first few days of withdrawal after years and years of heavy drinking. It would be entertaining for most of you and possibly instructive for a few of you out there who have just a little too much curiosity about what that's like (and you know who you are).

But since this is a book about truth, I can't provide that. It's not like I came home from the hospital and said, "OK, not only am I going to stop drinking for a while, I'm going to stop for years and years and write a book about what it's like to quit without going to Betty Ford or attending AA meetings."

Instead, I just came back to my apartment and stopped drinking. I didn't do anything dramatic—not right away, anyway. The vodka bottle in my fridge stayed there for about 30 days before I finally decided to dump it down the drain.

There were a few Michelob Ultras in the door of my fridge for maybe a year that Megan had brought over for herself one night and then never got around to drinking. It's not like seeing them there every time I opened the door had any chilling effect on me. They're just beer (and not very good beer at that).

My biggest worry, without question, was sleeping. You grow accustomed to drinking yourself to sleep night after night—either passing out on the couch or drinking enough that you just stumble into bed without any real memory of it—and the notion of going to bed cold sober is frightening. Scarier than it should be, as it turns out.

After two, maybe three nights of a lot of tossing and turning, I actually started to get good quality sleep by the end of the first week. It was like making this whole new discovery that you could actually go to bed and sleep for six or seven hours and feel refreshed in the morning.

Imagine that. Who knew?

One concern that remained—one I haven't mentioned to this point and still exists on a limited basis today—was the injury to my skull. There is a ridge along the back of the right side of my head that isn't supposed to be there. It's an indentation about two inches long. I can put three fingers of my right hand in the crevice or alongside it and feel the damage I did to my head that Christmas night.

That's just kind of a novelty really. It doesn't do any harm. I don't think.

But when I lie down and roll over and the right side of my head hits the pillow, the room tends to spin. Today it only spins for a second and stops. In those first few months after the injury, when I suffered one seizure and was possibly in danger of having another, it would spin for several seconds. It was uncomfortable to the point of being nauseating.

Basically, it felt a little like the room spinning when you're really drunk, but it felt more like when you're outside in the hot sun bending over and you rise up real quickly. That kind of spinning. That kind of dizziness. Sometimes I would grab the bed or the headboard to try to limit the motion.

That has not gone away over the years, but it doesn't happen all the time and it's of a much shorter duration now. Still—it's a lasting reminder of the stupidity I showed on Dec. 25, 2008.

Drinking to the point where you lose your balance and crack your skull open—I don't recommend it.

* * *

The next step in "not drinking" was one that's actually scary for a lot of drinkers. And that is, simply, telling friends you aren't drinking any more or, at the very least, you aren't drinking tonight.

How this news is received by people, even relatives or your closest friends, can be surprising.

Let's put it this way. If you've seen ESPN's Jon Barry, the former player and son of Rick Barry, give that "what the hell is that" look while announcing a game or doing studio work—he does it a lot if you watch him—well, that's the same look he gave me during the 2011 NBA Finals when he asked me what I wanted at the W hotel bar and I said, "O'Doul's."

Barry had been out with me several times on visits to Dallas but not in the last two seasons. In 2008 and early 2009 when he was here, needless to say, I wasn't ordering any O'Doul's.

It's not his fault or anyone else's that you get a lot of strange looks. I suppose if you were used to eating steaks and hamburgers with someone and you suddenly ordered a salad and declared yourself a vegetarian, you might get the same response. But whatever the dangers of eating too much red meat might be, changing that habit and stopping drinking to avoid killing someone else behind the wheel of a car or killing yourself through liver damage are two distinctly different things.

I'm sure it's different in each case, but most of my friends were extremely supportive. Maybe disingenuous, too, because I still don't understand all the "congratulations" I receive for stopping drinking from people who express no desire to be on the receiving end of such applause. But that's OK. I mostly think people congratulate you for not drinking because it's awkward and they have no idea what to say.

And as many times as I have told some of them, "Hey, it's OK if you have a beer or a few drinks around me, that's not going to bother me," most do not believe it. Or at least they feel the best way to show support is to stop drinking around me, which is entirely unnecessary.

I don't see a beer mug—even a lovely pilsner glass filled to the rim with Stella—and start craving one. I don't see a cocktail glass filled with vodka and get the shakes. And I sure as hell don't develop any desire for alcohol from seeing drunks doing shots.

I still go to bars to meet friends but do it less frequently. Here's the funny thing about bars I never knew.

They are filled with really annoying drunk people. Who would have guessed such a thing?

* * *

Don't get me wrong now. I don't want to make it sound like I came home from the hospital after that seizure and just kicked alcohol's ass like it had never been beaten before. There were challenges.

There are challenges.

Travel—which had lost maybe 50 percent of its charm over the years for any number of reasons including all the miseries heaped on travelers after 9-11—isn't something I embrace at all at this stage.

On the last day of the NFL regular season each year, you can determine a team's road trips for the coming season - not the dates, of course, but the cities which, in two cases, are based on the standings. In the press box for the Cowboys-Giants game, David Moore—the bon vivant and wine connoisseur of the *Dallas Morning News* staff—was trying to determine whether he preferred the Cowboys locking up a trip to San Francisco or Seattle.

I told him, "Yeah, I can't decide in which city I want to ignore people and stay in my room."

I was half-kidding. Maybe not even half.

The nights I've had in San Francisco, in New York, in Chicago provide a lifetime of great memories. Sure, there were a few slip-ups, a couple of missed flights, a night too drunk at Scoma's at the bar to even make it to dinner but let's not dwell on the negative. Mostly, those nights provided good memories, and it's important to note that because I suppose anyone could eventually figure out they need to stop drinking if every night was misery.

Most nights weren't. That's the hard part. Most nights were good. Some of them were great.

But the awful and the dangerous far outweigh everything else by now. So those nights have to be over for me. And I'm OK with that.

But a trip to New York is far different from what it was five years ago. That doesn't make it bad. I was far more excited in September, 2011, going to the U.S. Open for the first time, seeing Roger Federer and Novak Djokovic play a magical five-set semifinal than I had been about any night of eating and drinking in Manhattan for years.

That's the way it should be for me, and that's the way it is.

Drunk on sports all over again, just like a seven-year old in New Jersey whose mom has just bought him two packs of baseball cards for ten cents.

That was the best high there ever was. I'm still searching for it.

CHAPTER 14

JUST ME AND JOSH HAMILTON

"Sometimes I think of things and wonder
why I never thought of them before.
Sometimes I remember things and beg for mercy."

—*The People of Forever Are Not Afraid*
by Shani Boianjiu

THE TACO JOINT on Peak St. near Gaston Ave. doesn't look like much. Tucked into a tiny strip center between a Unisex salon and a Shamrock Station, it looks like, well, it looks like a taco joint. But if you're anywhere near downtown Dallas, it's the place to be on a hangover Saturday morning.

I was three months into this current journey towards sobriety. But that removed just one reason for wanting to be at the Taco Joint, not all of them. So I was sitting there, on vacation from the *Morning News* and reading the newspaper, not thinking there was any reason my life was about to take its most dramatic turn in the next 48 hours.

My phone buzzed with an 860 number. If ESPN doesn't own that entire area code in Connecticut, it comes damn close. The two previous years, my phone buzzed all the time with 860 numbers, calls from production assistants and others affiliated with *NASCAR Now*. After my untimely dismissal from that fine show, I wasn't getting many calls from the network (the *Around the Horn* production crew is in Washington), but I figured I would finish my tacos and check the voicemail a few minutes later.

I hadn't turned on a TV or listened to the radio or checked my twitter feed or anything else that morning. As I said, I was taking some vacation from the *Morning News* so a brief personal escape from the 24-hour news cycle seemed within reason.

When I got to my car, I listened to the message. A male voice said:

"Tim, we were just wondering if any chance you were with the Rangers in Anaheim, we could get you on ESPN News later today to talk about Josh Hamilton and the Deadspin story and photos. Thanks, give us a call."

Oops.

If you were a betting man, what's the percent chance you would give that Deadspin had just decided to do a positive article on Josh's recovery from addiction, complete with, oh, I don't know, maybe some pleasant family photos?

Would that be 1 percent? Or .001 percent?

* * *

Within a couple of hours, I had seen the photos of young women—alas, none of them named Katie Hamilton, devoted wife and mother of his children—licking Josh's bare chest in a Tempe, Ariz. bar. Hamilton's story of recovery was probably the most well known in all of sports.

No. 1 pick of the 1999 draft by Tampa Bay Devil Rays. Spends three years completely out of baseball addicted to crack. Fights his way back into reinstatement, plays one year in Cincinnati in 2007, then lights up the American League with the Rangers in 2008 with the greatest Home Run Derby performance of all time at Yankee Stadium.

Hamilton already had a book out called *Beyond Belief*, detailing his rise and fall and rise again in which he gives all the glory to Jesus Christ and the faith of his wife and his grandmother.

Although the relapse had happened before spring training, the story did not break for six months. He was still being drug tested three times a week and there were no indications then or now that he did any drugs the night of his relapse in Tempe. Certainly he did not fail a drug test afterwards.

Still, this was a huge story for obvious reasons. Even though injuries had limited him in 2009, 2.4 million fan votes made him an All-Star Game starter, anyway (he would get an MLB record 11 million for the 2012 Game). His appeal went not only beyond the Rangers fans base but beyond the normal sports fan base to include countless others battling alcohol and drug problems.

I watched on the news as Hamilton handled the questions about his slip-up better than most athletes handle questions about why they threw an interception. This was not a surprise. Hamilton has done countless interviews and testimonials and speeches about his recovery.

For him, this was a battle he lost one night in Arizona. It was a shameful experience and he felt terrible for his wife, his teammates, and his fans around the world. But it wasn't the end of the fight that he will proudly wage the rest of his life.

I thought a lot that night about Josh Hamilton, even though the two of us were not remotely close even in a sportswriter-athlete type way. When I walked into to the Rangers' clubhouse in 2009, it was customary to sit and chat with Michael Young, Marlon Byrd, Ian Kinsler, Derek Holland, Hank Blalock or Gerald Laird.

Josh wasn't on the list. Although I had written bits and pieces about his battles with addiction in columns, I had never interviewed him on the subject. I hadn't read his book, either.

Ten years earlier, when I briefly entertained the thought that maybe, just maybe, I had a drinking problem, I read Pete Hamill's *A Drinking Life* and Carolyn Knapp's *Drinking: A Love Story.*

Both great books I would recommend to anyone. Both books that I thought a lot about...

For a while.

In recent years, I had given less time for reflection. And even when a subject like Hamilton's addiction fell right into my lap—it's not like he played in Seattle—I tended to shy away.

Now seemed like a good time to stop pretending that Hamilton's tale was his alone. If a kid in his 20s with so much talent could be so damn open about his considerable flaws, why couldn't a guy in his 50s come to terms with his weaknesses and be honest with his readers?

Would it kill me to tell people that drinking nearly killed me?

On Sunday morning, I called Gary Leavell, the sports editor who handles the columnist assignments. I was relieved that I got his voice mail because—strange as it might sound—I wasn't quite ready to talk to other people about what I planned to write for all to read.

I left him a message, saying I wasn't down to write for a couple more days but I wanted to write a column about Josh in the Monday paper, anyway, and that it was going to be about both of us and it would include my drinking problem along with his addiction, sort of making fun of myself along the way as I compared the two of us, his baseball swing, my golf swing...

I'm sure the message rambled on for a bit. On a good day, when I try to explain my column subject to anyone, I articulate it very poorly. It's not until I sit down to write that I know exactly what I'm trying to say.

And now, just 90 days since my last drink—barely halfway to my personal record—I was going to tell friends, family and the readers of the *Dallas Morning News* that I had a serious drinking problem that I had managed to keep hidden for most of my adult life.

I knew what I wanted to do, but I hadn't thought much about the reaction or the possible consequences.

When I finally sat down to type Sunday afternoon, it came out like this...

* * *

Published: August 10, 2009

I want to believe Josh Hamilton but not because I'm a die-hard Rangers fan. When I enter the Rangers clubhouse, he's not one of the four or five guys I tend to talk to every visit.

But when I see Hamilton look sincerely apologetic about his drinking binge in January, when I listen to him say it hasn't happened in those seven months since and that this was his one and only slip-up in nearly four years of recovery from addiction, I want to believe in him.

Because I want to believe in me.

When you think about it, Josh and I are pretty much the same guy other than two things. He is covered with tattoos and has a million dollar thing-of-beauty baseball swing.

I once wanted to get a Top Cat tattoo in Austin, but my daughter wouldn't let me, and I have a $2 thing-of-ugly golf swing.

Other than that, hey, just a couple of guys who when they stop in a bar for a drink, their pictures pop up on Web sites. (Mine show up on the really slow news days).

Hamilton watched more than three years of his professional career sail by during his darkest days of battling drugs and alcohol.

I watched the Cowboys lose to the Eagles, 44-6, last December from my room at Parkland Hospital after suffering a fractured skull of undetermined origin.

When Josh says he's foggy on the details of his drinking in Arizona, I'm right there with him in the fog. How I got into an ambulance to go to Parkland will remain one of my life's little mysteries.

That's what happens when you have a blood alcohol level of .26.

I do want to mention that I wasn't driving that night. I wish I could report that I stopped drinking after that incident.

I'd like to say that having those staples and stitches removed from the back of my head with no anesthetic was painful enough to teach me a lesson I should have learned the first time my kids asked, "Daddy, why are you drinking?"

But, as is the case with Josh and millions of others, it took a whole series of incidents and lessons before anything meaningful began to win the battle against denial.

My Parkland doctor even told me that despite a sound recovery from the fractured skull, seizures were possible in the next nine months. Excessive drinking could even trigger them.

I figured that seizures were things that happened to losers. Besides, I had a lot of stress at work (the catch-all excuse that works for everyone).

On May 7, I got another ride in an ambulance. This one I actually remember. We had just about finished an episode of *The Ben and Skin Show* on 105.3 The Fan when I hit the deck, having suffered my first (and hopefully last) seizure.

Troy Hughes, the board operator and a former Eagle Scout, swung into action, pouncing on me and making sure I didn't swallow my tongue. I'm not completely sure this was necessary, I think Troy always had a thing for me, but let's go with his story.

Ben and Skin accompanied me to the emergency room. To be honest, they did some of their best work there.

At this point—perhaps fearful of missing what few episodes of that underrated radio show remained—I decided to stop drinking for a while.

I have never been to rehab or an AA meeting—although I know people whose lives have been turned around by one or the other—but have read enough and I know enough not to say "I stopped drinking for good."

I can't even say that's necessarily the goal. I would like to be that distinguished gentleman who can have two glasses of red wine with a nice steak and stop drinking for the rest of the night, but I have my doubts.

One, I'm not totally certain that guy exists other than in commercials. Two, I much prefer vodka to wine, and two glasses is like a warm-up act. Three, in the first three decades of my drinking career I was never that guy so I'm not totally confident he's in my future.

So, we're at three months without a drink now, but who's counting? I haven't done anything heroic by any stretch of the imagination. I have simply tried to understand my life and get it in order.

In the same way, I certainly don't think of Hamilton as any kind of hero although he is viewed in that manner by the millions of baseball fans who voted him a starting outfielder in the All-Star Game. I know Hamilton doesn't look at himself in that light.

He has to fight drugs beyond alcohol, which I and many others do not. Maybe that means he has more demons to slay. But a hero?

He's a guy who came this close to throwing away athletic gifts only a select few can imagine.

He's a human who, in recovery, is trying to make the most of his life for his family and friends and, as a professional athlete, his teammates.

The fact that he lost a battle last January does nothing to diminish what he's trying to accomplish.

He might hope to win a World Series or a home run title. He might hope to sign a long-term, mega-million dollar contract. But that's not Josh Hamilton's ultimate goal.

His goal is the same as lots of people reading this. It's the same as millions more whose thoughts and actions are controlled by alcohol or drugs rather than the other way around.

It's the same as mine.

He's trying to live.

—Copyright 2009 *The Dallas Morning News*

* * *

After I sent the column to the *Morning News* that afternoon, I got another voicemail from Leavell later that day (if it sounds like I only communicate with other humans through text messages and voicemails, that's basically true). This one said he loved it, but that the paper was prepared to pull it late that night if I decided that it was too personal and that I didn't want it to run.

I thanked him but didn't really give it a second thought. I wanted the story to be out there. I wanted my daughter, two weeks away from leaving for Mizzou, to see it. I wanted my son, about a month short of starting high school, to see it. I wanted my dad and all of his friends in AA to see it.

I wanted people who didn't know me but who would be surprised that something like this could happen to someone who was enjoying success in the newspaper-TV world to see it.

I wanted to put some real pressure on myself to stay sober. As long as I was just playing this personal game—90 days and counting without a drink—I could revert to form at any time. I even wondered if they were starting to miss me at the three liquor stores that I used on a rotating basis. Doesn't every drunk have a three-store rotation? I used two just off I-35 and one in the Uptown area closer to where I lived so that I didn't need to buy a fifth of vodka from any of them more than once every two weeks.

Clever, huh?

And so the column ran. And the reaction was beyond anything that I could have imagined.

* * *

I write columns on the Cowboys that generate 20, 30, maybe 50 emails. I write columns some days that only get one or two. In general, I get fewer comments than I did five years ago, possibly because there are fewer readers but mostly because they can comment on blogs, they can see it on my twitter and Facebook pages. They just have more ways to respond if they feel like it.

I got more than 300 emails when I wrote about me and Josh, just a couple of good ol' country boy athletes (minus the country and athlete part on my half) with drinkin' problems.

I got text messages of support from Michael Young, from Jon Daniels, from golf guru Hank Haney who was a downtown Dallas neighbor then, and from media members, some of them friends, some not so much.

To be honest, it was more than I expected and a little more than I wanted. I kept reading emails from strangers saying, "We wish you the best in your battle with addiction," and "We are praying for you tonight."

Wait. Timeout. I didn't ask to be in your prayers. I'm not even in my own prayers. I don't pray!

I didn't even claim to be an addict. I left the door open just a crack to be that guy who can have the two glasses of wine in his favorite booth at Bob's.

(NOTE: I saw my physician about three months after the column appeared and we talked about it. He said, "You know where you said you might be one of those people who can have a drink or two and be all right? I don't think you're one of those people.")

In addition to the overwhelming support, I did hear from a few people who said I was out of line. "You're writing about this after three months? Try 13 years," one of them wrote.

Well, I hadn't said I was cured or that three months was a significant hurdle, I was just putting it out there as a starting point.

Others said I had no chance without turning my life over to Jesus Christ. Others said without the support group of AA, I would never make it. A few said if I had not yet been to rehab, I couldn't consider myself to be recovering from anything.

I certainly didn't argue with these people when I responded to their emails. They may, in time, prove to be correct.

But if AA or religion or rehab had the answers for everyone, they would be batting 1.000. And we all know that they are not.

Hamilton's book offers just one example of a person in which rehab failed time after time.

I was just beginning the search to find what would work best for me. I heard over and over again that you can't do this alone, but again, that's based on others' experiences, the cries for help that emanate from somebody else's problems.

By nature, I am not a joiner of clubs. I do not read self-help books. My plan—if you can even call it so much as a plan—was to start alone with the help of friends and family and see if that weren't enough.

Hell, I'd almost thrown it all away on a drunken Christmas night at the end of a year in which, between the *Morning News* and two shows with ESPN, I made over $400,000.

I'm a math-brain guy. If I couldn't figure out from a personal standpoint what my love affair with vodka was doing to me, I should be able to crunch the numbers and determine what it nearly cost me.

But I appreciated the outpouring of emails and the text messages far more than anything else I had ever felt when being congratulated on a good column. And it had the intended effect of putting my daily battle out there in the public eye.

Regardless of whether I was going to learn from AA or find religion or seek help from anyone else along the way, my struggle was no longer just a personal one.

If I started drinking again, it wasn't just a few friends and bartenders in Dallas that were going to notice. My effort to quit was no longer something I could just quit.

* * *

When I flew out to Arizona for a few days of Rangers spring training in March, 2010, I had determined that I needed to talk to Josh. It wasn't so much for a column as it was for a chapter in a book I was starting to write. And it was also to talk about my experiences as much as his—if he was interested.

I shouldn't have been surprised that he was.

By this time I had read his book including the updated chapter about his relapse in 2009. Although I had jokingly referred to our similarities in my column, the important differences seemed striking at first.

Hamilton's addiction cost him millions of dollars for three years during what should have been the early prime of his career. I was a functioning alcoholic for years, for a time holding down the equivalent of two full-time jobs.

When Hamilton drank, he inevitably would move on to crack cocaine. I was way too old for the drug scene, or at least I thought I was until the news about Rangers manager Ron Washington broke later that spring.

Hamilton had visions of demons in cloud formations while playing in the minors. After he had lost everything, he had vivid dreams of winning a major league home-run derby and being interviewed by a female reporter on the field and talking about his having been saved by Jesus Christ.

I never really had any visions or dreams that I saw in terms of foreshadowing my future. I think I would laugh them off if I did.

But the more I read, the more I recognized that the differences were not as significant as the similarities. We both drank to escape something even if we couldn't always define what it was.

He would stop for weeks or months at a time and then fall back into the same destructive behavior. Me? Heck, I've quit drinking more times than I can remember.

And when Hamilton had his relapse in 2009, by God if he didn't have a few vodka cranberries that sent him down the wrong path.

Been there. Drank that.

We stood outside the clubhouse one afternoon, hours before a Rangers spring training night game, and talked about the oddly similar lives that a slugger and a writer could lead when alcohol takes over.

I told Josh I was surprised by how many emails I had received from people saying how disappointed they were in him after his relapse. As if it was just a decision he made one day to get drunk in a bar in Tempe, Ariz.

"People don't understand," Hamilton said. "It's something that my wife told me after I relapsed. I came in the house and she said, 'I'm sick of it.' I said, 'Sick of what?'

"She said, 'I'm sick of people saying, I love you, but I'm disappointed, embarrassed, blah, blah, blah. People that really love you should just say, I love you.'

"And that really hit home with me. People don't realize the struggle that people who battle alcohol and drug addiction go through. We're one bad decision from being right back where we were. And when they happen—it's not a quick decision."

Hamilton believes the source of his trouble is when he starts to take sobriety and his Christian faith for granted. That's why he doesn't mind telling his story over and over whether it's for a visiting writer, a youth group or, occasionally, a total stranger.

"I don't think it's a burden. It's a privilege for me to tell my story," he said. "It's part of what I do to stay sober— getting in the Bible, praying. When I get away from that, that's when thoughts start coming in my head about drinking."

I asked him if he felt like he got screwed by the Deadspin story, if he felt he wouldn't be better off living in an era without camera phones and the insatiable desire to bring celebrities crashing down to the ground.

"It's kind of mixed, really, but I'm glad to be held accountable on a national level," he said. "Sometimes you look at your teammates and you say, 'Damn, they can have a couple beers, surely I can go do that, too.' But once I get one in, I'll have two, three, four and then I don't stop."

One way to avoid drinking: Hamilton still doesn't carry more than $20 in his pocket. Incredible when you think about the major league per diem of more than $80 per day.

"When I relapsed, I had taken the safeguards out of place. I had a credit card with me, and I couldn't get cash out with it, but I had it in case I needed gas. I had been in Arizona for three weeks, working out hard, lifting, in great shape. I thought I could have one drink and I went to a little pizza parlor in Tempe.

"Well, you know, one leads to 10 and you don't remember half of what you do. I felt like I'd let God down, my wife and family down, my teammates. The nation, really."

That's serious accountability when you've got your 2.4 million All-Star voters pulling for you.

"People come up to me and say they read my book. I say, 'That's great, you read it, but what did you learn from it?'" he said.

Josh asked me what I wanted my book to say.

I told him that I thought most of the stories about people's battles with drugs and alcohol come from the rich and famous. Even though I have achieved a modest level of fame compared to most, you don't have to be that Hollywood star or that completely out-of-control drug user to have a serious problem that may be ruining your life and others as well.

You don't always have to be the drunkest guy in the room to be the guy with a serious problem.

We talked about AA meetings. I said I had thought about them but wasn't interested in going yet. He said they only made him crave a drink although he was quick to say he knows how important AA is in many people's lives and he would never criticize it. It just wasn't for him.

I figured at some point Josh was going to ask me about Jesus. I'm not a big believer in organized religion and my children are Jewish, but it's like AA or, for that matter, soccer or *American Idol*.

I know this stuff works for millions of people. It's just not there for me, at least not now.

But Josh was great about it when the subject finally came up.

"All I can tell you is that it's what works for me. I go to a non-denominational church. I read the Bible. When you accept Jesus Christ, Satan comes at you a lot harder because now he's got something to lose," he said.

I don't know about the Satan stuff. Neither do those that think they do.

But we all use whatever tools we can get our hands on in order to deal with our problems. I respect Josh's view and the way he sees life. As for me, I'm hanging on to the notion that Josh and I are just different versions of the same story that others can learn from.

* * *

Of course, Josh's story took another turn in Feb, 2012, when it was reported that he had another night of drinking in a Dallas bar. I was at the Super Bowl in Indianapolis at the time. In fact, we were just getting ready to talk about Hamilton in the first segment of *Around the Horn* Friday when an ESPN production assistant walked into the room where we were taping and said that in addition to ribs being out for lunch, there was also tequila, Capt. Morgan rum and Crown Royal on the table.

Well—it was, after all, the Super Bowl.

I thought Hamilton did a nice job of facing the music—again—but his story had some holes in it. He said he had three or four drinks with a friend and then called Ian Kinsler, but when Kinsler got to the restaurant, he didn't tell Kinsler he had been drinking.

Anyone—and that includes Josh—who says "three or four" means "five or more." But even if it had been four drinks, Kinsler, who sees Hamilton sober every day during the baseball season, couldn't tell Josh had been drinking?

Regardless, it was another night in which Hamilton lost the battle. He wins most of the time, but this isn't a game where even a .990 batting average gets the job done.

This is the longest game. There's no bottom of the ninth and no finish line.

Hamilton's Rangers career ended unceremoniously with a dropped fly ball on a too casual attempt against Oakland, and a completely hapless 0-for-4 in the wild card game with Baltimore.

Some would say Hamilton bounced back nicely from that sluggish finish by signing a $125 million guaranteed contract with the Angels.

And that's true enough. But for Hamilton and his battles with addiction, or for any of us who have landed in this struggle, life is batting practice that never ends. Success means just getting to take another turn in the cage.

CHAPTER 15

SELF-SUFFICIENT ILLUSION

"My life is really different than it was.
I live alone. I'm bored a lot more.
I'm really grateful for this boring life of mine."

—Kate (Mary Elizabeth Winstead) in *Smashed*

I REMEMBER THE awkwardness of my stepmother handing my dad a glass of champagne when my son Ben was born at Baylor Hospital on Jan. 9, 1995. Willis was a little more than a year into sobriety. For him, two AA meetings per week was already the norm.

I'm pretty sure the next to last thing he wanted at that moment was a glass of champagne. But the last thing he wanted was to incur Patricia's wrath, so I think he took the smallest sip possible.

But what exactly is the proper celebration for sobriety?

We celebrate everything else with shots, with champagne, with forgettable and (often regrettable) toasts. But how best to celebrate a life newly devoted to—the avoidance of nightly celebrations?

On May 9, 2010—one year after my seizure and "third strike," Megan said she wanted to take me out to eat. Anywhere I wanted to go. We were barely going out at that point as she was ready to get on with her life. Our 24-year age difference was never the factor people assume such a gap has to produce. Steely Dan's lyrics to *Hey Nineteen* (as in "That's Aretha Franklin, she don't remember Queen of Soul") never applied. As a matter of fact, Steely Dan was her favorite band when we met. How many 27-year-olds can you say that about?

But she was pushing 31 now—ancient by her standards—and ready to get married, start a family and do all the other things I could not accommodate. She was about to move on, and I cannot fault her for that (although I'm pretty sure I tried). Even if we weren't really going out on a regular basis, the first year of sobriety was made easier by her presence in my life. And I thank her for that.

She took me to Cyclon Anaya's, a kind of upscale Tex-Mex place on Oak Lawn. A couple of years before, going there for a couple of margaritas at the bar, then some sangria (to slow the pace a bit) during dinner on the patio would have been the perfect start to a great evening.

Or a perfect start to an evening about to go terribly wrong. One never knows about these things.

Instead, I was fine drinking iced tea and, I believe, one non-alcoholic beer. It was a good evening, not great. Hey, in this life "good" is good enough. It's one of the most difficult things to learn, but once you accept that those great highs can only be accompanied by an equal number of miserable and sometimes disastrous, even deadly lows, a "good" time is more than just ok.

For a more extensive celebration of the one-year anniversary of being free of alcohol's grip, I decided to watch some drunks on film. I wanted to see what if anything I was missing. No, that's not quite right.

I wanted to see a portrayal of miserable drunks in movies. That was the intent. What I got was one of the most miserable portrayals of a drunk, one that was unfathomably rewarded with a Best Actor Oscar in 1995.

I rented three movies—*Sideways*, *Barfly* and *Leaving Las Vegas*.

The only one I hadn't seen was *Sideways* and I was a bit misinformed as to what it was. Yes, Paul Giamatti and his buddy, Thomas Haden Church, drink a lot of wine and occasionally make poor decisions on an inebriated tour of the wine country.

But these aren't the drunks I know. I spent those two years covering the Giants and enjoyed the three or four visits to the wine country that my young wife, Lori, and I made there, but I have lived in Texas the past 23 years and for most of my life. This is the land of beer drinkers and shot takers.

This is not wine-sipping country.

Next I watched *Barfly* which I remembered as being good but wasn't sure how good. Who knows? There's a pretty good chance I was drinking the first time I watched it at home, don't you think?

It's impressive that an actor such as Mickey Rourke, who's not exactly afraid to overdo it or steal a scene, can get a drunk so accurately at the same time. I think drunks are diffi-cult to play on TV or in film. Most actors get it wrong, slur-ring words or wobbling across the screen.

(If you want to see two people who get it right time after time, watch Amy Poehler and especially Rashida Jones on one of my favorite shows, *Parks and Recreation*. They do it a lot, and they nail it every time.)

Now you might be cynical and suggest Rourke was just playing himself. How much credit does a man who's led such a wheels-off life get for playing a wheels-off character? Re-gardless, there are many great moments, and much of it is a tribute to the screenplay, not just Rourke's performance.

Henry (Rourke) spends most of the movie getting beat up by Eddie (Frank Stallone of all people) and hanging out with fellow barfly Wanda (Faye Dunaway). I've seen people that maintain the perpetual half-drunkenness of Henry, able to function enough to get to the bar, to occasionally pay for their drinks but not quite capable of functioning in society.

"I can't stand people," Wanda tells him when they first meet at the bar. "I hate them. Do you hate them?"
Henry: "No—but I seem to feel better when they're not around."

Henry delivers all of his little speeches in the film in the same sing-song style.

On why he doesn't stop drinking: "Anybody can do that. Anybody can be a non-drinker. It takes a special talent to be a drunk. It takes ENDURANCE. Endurance is more impor-tant than truth."

On not having a job: "You know somebody laid down this rule where everybody's got to DO something, everybody's got to BE somebody—a dentist, a glider pilot, a narc, a janitor, a preacher. Sometimes I just get tired of thinking all the things I don't wanna DO, all the things I don't wanna BE, all the places I don't wanna GO, like India. Like getting my teeth cleaned."

Near the end, the woman who's trying to encourage Henry's work as a writer says that being a drunk "seems like a limited world, is there anything else to it?"

Henry responds, "No. Just self-sufficient illusion."

Although the fights look like Hollywood fights, there's never a single moment in the bar, The Golden Horn ("A Friendly Place"), that comes across as unreal. There's never a shot where I think Rourke is anything but a genuine drunk.

Maybe I haven't known people quite as destitute as Henry and Wanda. But I've certainly met a few just this side of desperate, folks whose local bar was their home away from home and for them, sadly, it was a happier place than their home. At least that's how they envisioned the bar at the start of each day.

On the other hand, there's not a single minute in *Leaving Las Vegas* where I found Nicolas Cage to be remotely believable as a drunk. The manner in which he takes huge gulps from liquor bottles, the things he says as he moves inexorably towards drinking himself to death don't contain an ounce of truth.

I remembered thinking the movie was overrated when I saw it in a theater and wondering how he and this film possibly could have been so honored at the time. You can argue the idiocy of *Dances With Wolves* over *GoodFellas* for best picture but I'll put Cage winning an Oscar for this mess right alongside them.

As he slowly drinks himself to death, you feel nothing. As for Elisabeth Shue, you just feel sorry that this was the best role she could get. Given her recent work in *Piranha*, maybe it's just not going to happen for her.

It was painful to watch, not because Cage reminded me of myself or anyone I'd ever known. I just felt bad for all the other actors in 1995 who watched him collect a Golden Globe and an Oscar for this portrayal.

Nobody who's ever had a drinking problem has willfully chosen to be like Rourke's character. But there's an understanding of how a life can descend to that level and how, once having reached the bottom, the escape route doesn't seem worth searching for. Rourke captures it. Cage swings for the fences and misses by a mile.

At least that was my appraisal one year removed from drinking as I searched for my past in the eyes of others.

Chapter 16

AROUND THE HORN TAKES AN UNEXPECTED TURN

"The less we say about it the better
We'll make it up as we go along
Feet on the ground
Head in the sky
It's OK, I know nothing's wrong…nothing."

—*This Must Be the Place* by Talking Heads

HAVE I MENTIONED that we do a one-hour conference call at 9:30 Central time every day that *Around the Horn* is on the air?

Have I mentioned how many times I came up with bogus excuses—"Hey, I gotta finish this column early today"—to avoid the 1-hour call and just get the show's topics in about a five-minute call with producer Aaron Solomon around 11 a.m.? All in order to gain an extra 90 minutes of sleep after a night of drinking?

Well, I didn't count the number of times I did it between the time the show was born in late 2002 and I stopped drinking in 2009. Let's say it was 20 times (a bit on the low side) and leave it at that.

Once sobriety was a regular feature of my mornings, I stopped making those excuses. I felt fortunate that I had survived on the show as long as I had undetected—or if undetected is the wrong word, I was pleased that my drinking never knocked me off the show, even if e-mailers or, by early 2009, twitter followers would comment on my look on certain days.

Eventually, a brush with the law would forever change *Around the Horn* in 2010. But it wouldn't be mine.

It was on a Saturday morning in August, 2010, that I got a text message on my phone from a producer. The text advised me not to comment on "Jay's situation."

I didn't even know what Jay's situation was until I sat down at my laptop. Given Mariotti's never-ending war with Deadspin, The Big Lead and bloggers of all types, I suspected the information would not be hard to find.

It wasn't.

Ironically, Mariotti had used his "facetime" in a show about a year earlier to talk about Lil Wayne's arrest and sentence since Lil Wayne had made an appearance on *Around the Horn* earlier in 2009. "If you had Jay Mariotti in 'the first *Around the Horn* panelist to go to jail' pool, you were wrong," Jay said.

It was one of his better lines. It wasn't quite accurate, but then no one knew about my arrest in '07.

The details of Mariotti's two arrests in California on domestic violence charges that led to his no-contest plea, his five years' probation, community service, counseling—this information is all over the Internet if you want to read about it now.

But I got a call that day from the show's executive producer, Erik Rydholm, who created *PTI* and who spends about 18 hours a day getting *PTI* and *Around the Horn* (and now also Dan LeBetard's *Highly Questionable*) on the air. And Rydholm was great. He didn't tell any of us what to say about Jay. He simply said that this thing was going to have to play its way out before Jay's status could be determined.

All I can say now is that Mariotti, like the rest of us (except for Paige who, for a time, had his own contract), was always day-to-day on the show. That's how we get paid and that's how the schedule comes out each week. We let Solomon, another unseen but invaluable part of the show, know our availability and each Thursday he sends out the following week's schedule.

In that sense, it truly is "the show of competitive banter" as 10 or 11 panelists jockey for 20 spots each week.

And that's how Mariotti, who had been on more shows than anyone, disappeared in 2010. A man who once did 265 consecutive shows—now there's a sports record that will never be broken—simply vanished from public view. The baggage that came with his alleged assault on a woman was just too much of a load for the show to carry when it didn't have to.

This book is about me being honest about everything in my life. So while I'm not out to trash anyone else, I can't say with any degree of honesty that I think Jay's departure has been a bad thing for anyone other than him.

Did I hope it would lead to more shows for me? Of course I did. I just told you we get paid by the show. Three shows a week is better than two, and when Mariotti got arrested, each show was worth $1000 to the panelists.

Has working on the show become more of a pleasure than it was prior to August, 2010? Absolutely.

Those in Washington D.C. where the show is written, shot and produced feel likewise, but I won't speak for them. Other than one exchange of text messages after his arrest, I have had no contact with him. I really didn't know what to say to Jay that day because one thing the man can certainly do is detect bullshit. So I told him, hey, I have had some problems myself and they all got worked out so hopefully things would get better soon.

I didn't bother to say: Hey, I know how handcuffs feel too; I just kept it from ESPN better than you did.

Interestingly, when Mariotti was arrested, I received a text from Charles Barkley asking for Jay's number. Mariotti had been unsparing in his criticism of Barkley through the years (actually you could replace Barkley with any name you choose and this sentence remains accurate). But Jay was forever getting on Barkley for his gambling or for the controversial things he might say on TNT. Still, Barkley wanted to wish Jay the best of luck.

And I hope that Jay has managed to get his life together in recent years but I honestly wouldn't know if he has. He lives in LA but no one connected with the show is in regular contact with him.

Beyond that, I don't have any doubt that this show can go on without Woody, without Tony (that will be the hardest part) and certainly without me.

For now, it goes on with us. After opening with the Original Five White Guys from the Carnegie Deli meeting, the show added J.A. Adande, Kevin Blackistone and Jackie MacMullan in the first few months. In recent years, Bomani Jones, Israel Gutierrez, Jemele Hill and Pablo Torre have joined the mix.

In fact, Bill Plaschke, who joined the show in the spring of 2003, is the last white male to be added to the regular crew. A show that ignored diversity when it began can hardly be accused of doing so now. And it's a hell of a lot better show now than when it started out, too, not only because of the different faces and voices but, because through sheer repetition, some of us have gone from unwatchable to tolerable.

If I'm part of the reason for the show's success and staying power, maybe it's because of my encyclopedic sports knowledge. Or more likely it's because of my (unfortunately shelved) Al Davis impersonation.

But I also know that, since 2009, sitting down to tape a show three times a week without being exhausted from drinking the night before has something to do with it.

CHAPTER 17

LOOKING FOR A PURPOSE
FROM A NEON SIGN

"There was music in the cafes at night
and revolution in the air."

—*Tangled Up in Blue*, Bob Dylan

THE DECISION TO stop drinking brought an odd set of problems along with it. In this particular case, none of them are real. All of them mattered greatly.

While I always enjoyed having a drink in my hands while watching a sporting event (not the ones I was covering), alcohol had a strong connection to the songs and the films and the TV shows we all loved as well.

Take music first. Think of the songs, the albums you enjoyed most in college or during your 20s. Do you have a drink (or possibly a joint) in your hand in those memories? How do we continue to embrace the same music if we come out against the drinking that, in some ways, fueled our enjoyment and brought more magic to those songs?

Consider this. My political views tend to be all over the board, but if you had to label me, based on my voting record, I would be more liberal than conservative. And when I used to occasionally hear Rush Limbaugh's show come on the radio, the thing that bothered me more than any opinion he held was this:

How can he use a Pretenders song to introduce his show?

Chrissy Hynde and The Pretenders didn't sing anything that would remotely attach them to the Republican Party or the conservative movement. It seemed not only unfair but disingenuous.

So, for me, if so many of my memories of listening to Springsteen or Dylan or Steely Dan from college days were linked to having a Budweiser in one hand, how do I disassociate myself from one while staying connected to the other?

Hell, how am I supposed to sing "What a beautiful buzz, what a beautiful buzz" along with Mick in *Loving Cup* if there is no buzz?

There was a sense that, in confronting my problems with alcohol and making the absolutely right decision for me personally, I was joining the wrong team in the process. I don't want Carrie Nation and the Woman's Christian Temperance Union cheering for me from beyond the grave.

I don't want Mormons on bikes nodding their heads in approval, saying, "Way to go, Tim." Just the perception of a connection to the religious right is nearly enough to put a drink back in my hands.

I said nearly enough.

Beyond that, I think of all the people I've met who have claimed to never having had a drink. This would include several people in the sports media business and, well, Deion Sanders. Gotta be honest. Can't say I trust any of them.

Here's one thing I have thought about a lot in recent years. You don't have to be a sports reporter for very long before you run into athletes who "give all the glory to God" after every triumphant game. In the 70s and 80s, these athletes tended to fall under the heading of "born again Christians" although now I think so many athletes have simply recognized the escape hatch they create by wrapping themselves in the Bible that it goes way beyond those who are "born again."

Regardless, in my early days as a reporter, when I heard someone evoke Jesus' name, it troubled me greatly. I made the assumption that this particular athlete didn't drink as a result of his religious conversion. He seemed to be playing for a different team than the one I had so readily adopted.

But over time I actually realized it was the reverse that scared me the most. When I heard of someone quitting drinking—it didn't have to be an athlete, could have simply been someone I knew—my initial concern was that they were going to play the religion card, perhaps even try to persuade me to join their noble cause.

And I feel like I can even see that in people's eyes today when they are informed that I no longer drink. They study me for a moment. They wait for the next shoe to drop.

"So, Tim, you quit drinking because…?"

No. It wasn't that. My thoughts on religion have not changed. In fact, they remain one of the reasons that AA meetings have no place for me. They say they aren't a religion-based organization. So why do they meet so often in churches?

More importantly, I have this book called *Twenty-Four Hours a Day*. I'm pretty sure my father slipped it to me years ago and I just stuck it on a bookshelf, but as I type this I'm looking at it. The foreword says: *"Twenty-Four Hours a Day* is intended for members of Alcoholics Anonymous as a help in their program…"

There is a page for each day in the calendar year, and each contains a "Thought for the Day," "Meditation for the Day" and "Prayer for the Day."

Sorry. Not for me.

God didn't get me into this mess and he isn't getting false credit for getting me out of it.

Anyway, that's their business. They have their mythological figures to look up to, and so do I.

I'm not kidding you at all when I say I gave considerable thought to this when I stopped drinking:

How in the world was I going to watch *Mad Men* without a cocktail glass in my hand?

For the first two seasons of the AMC show, Megan and I watched many of the episodes together, drinks in hand. Thank God (see, I can give him/her credit when it's due) for the invention of the DVR. We frequently watched all or at least parts of shows of twice because when we got up the next morning, neither of us (especially me) could recall exactly how things had ended the night before for Don and Peggy and Joanie and Roger.

I could not even imagine watching the show while sipping on a Diet Coke. It just wouldn't feel right.

Mad Men was not alone in this regard. If part of me wanted to join Don Draper and Roger Sterling with a cocktail at an exclusive New York club, the other part definitely wanted to be out with McNulty and Bunk pounding a few beers and shots at a Baltimore dive bar.

The cops in *The Wire* drank. The cool ones drank a lot. Hell, I wanted to be at one of those police officer wakes where everyone is shit-faced but happy.

Drown my sorrows after a long day with a shot of whiskey with U.S. Marshall Raylan Givens of *Justified*? Just point me in the direction of Harlan County, Kentucky (hey, I know they film it in California) and I'm there—hoping to run into Boyd Crowder as well.

And, my gosh, the chance to walk into Paddy's pub and slam a few back with Max and Sweet Dee and Charlie and Dennis? How does anyone NOT want to be a regular part of *It's Always Sunny in Philadelphia*?

I don't limit my desires to drink with people to actors playing roles in my favorite TV shows. I can go animated if you like.

How do you not want to have Scotch and a few gummi bears with Sterling Mallory Archer? The modern version of James Bond may be a cartoon character on FX's *Archer*, but—in the spirit of Archer - A. The show is brilliant, B. I'm never going to get Lana into the sack without cocktails and C. Uhh, get back to me on C. I thought I had something there.

I could extend this chapter by about 5,000 words by listing all the cool people portrayed on TV and cinema who were shown to be serious drinkers. But I think you get the point.

Now let's move to the list of really cool characters that don't drink.

Well—there's Major Dick Winters of *Band of Brothers* brilliantly played by Damian Lewis, who's now portraying a very different military figure on *Homeland.*

I don't recall if it's ever explained in *Band of Brothers* why the major doesn't drink. His comrades poke fun at him at times even though his best friend, Capt. Nixon, has a huge alcohol problem that becomes a significant story line in one episode.

But since Winters was the real-life leader of Easy Company, that's different from deliberately creating a fictional character who doesn't drink.

Keeping that in mind, we have—Dr. Sheldon Cooper of *Big Bang Theory?*

The Emmy-winning Jim Parsons is terrific, but I'm not sure "cool" would come quickly to mind for anyone trying to describe that show's central character, a brilliant but socially inept theoretical physicist.

But I do want to give huge props to NBC's *Community,* a risk-taking comedy that deserved a bigger audience and better network treatment than it ever received. It made the closest thing I can think of to an anti-alcohol-without-being-preachy episode when Troy Barnes, the young African-American character played by Donald Glover, turned 21.

His older friends took him out for a night of drinking to celebrate. It went very badly for almost everyone involved, and Troy eventually chose not to get drunk and actually drove others home.

"Alcohol makes people sad," Barnes said. "It's like the Lifetime movies of beverages."

Thank you, Troy. Thank you, show creator Dan Harmon. This may not have qualified as one of the more memorable risks this sometimes bizarre show has taken in its first three seasons. But I won't forget it.

CHAPTER 18

WILD CARD

"Drinkin' don't bother my memory. If it did, I
wouldn't drink. I couldn't. You see, I'd forget how
good it was, then where would I be?"

—Eddie (Walter Brennan) in *To Have and Have Not*

BASEBALL HISTORY IS about to be made. In a little
more than one hour, the first American League one-game
wild card playoff will begin. The last few Orioles to take batting practice are getting their final swings. There are three
people standing behind the cage at home plate in Rangers
Ballpark—Orioles manager Buck Showalter, ESPN's Tim
Kurkjian and myself.

And it is moments like these that I cherish. That I know
I am truly lucky. That I am reminded of what it was like to be
drunk on sports at an early age before I became drunk on
something far more sinister for years as an adult.

There is, however, plenty of drinking in the story I am telling, a story Buck loves to hear but can't tell accurately because he doesn't remember much other than his jaw dropping to the floor when former GM John Hart spoke at the end of the night.

It's a story famous around the *Morning News* offices as "the Hicks dinner." In 2005, the Rangers tried to fix a contentious relationship that had built up between the team's upper management—primarily owner Tom Hicks, Hart, and Showalter—and the *Morning News* writers and columnists.

It had reached a point in the previous off-season that while Texas was trying to move Alex Rodriguez, first to the Red Sox and then eventually to the Yankees, Hicks wouldn't talk to beat writer Evan Grant. So I made the regular nightly calls to Hicks, then relayed what he said to Evan. The height of silliness.

Anyway, the Rangers invited several of us to dine with the club owner and officials to achieve some sort of détente. Because really, what could be more relaxing than dinner at a mansion, more than 32,000 square feet and appraised as the most valuable house in the city ($39 million) last time I checked.

The more memorable moments leading up to the main event were pitching coach Orel Hershiser telling us "I'd take a bullet for John Hart" and a 27-year-old soft-spoken assistant GM named Jon Daniels scolding us for not being more positive in our coverage of the club's Richard Hidalgo signing.

As the man who is now the most accomplished GM in the club's history has told me since, "I was just trying to get into the conversation. I should have kept my mouth shut."

But throughout the evening while the rest of us had spoken on any number of subjects, most of it just light-hearted chatter, John Hart had sat quietly at one end of the table. Hart was the subject of most media criticism after coming into Texas with guns blazing, making one ill-fated signing after another prior to the 2002 season—Chan Ho Park, John Rocker, the return of Juan Gonzalez.

I was seated near the middle of one long side of the table with Hicks on my immediate right. As dessert was served, Hicks noted that John had been quiet and asked if he would like to say a few words.

I can't tell you for sure if Hart had consumed more vodka than I had that night. I'm guessing he had but I won't put that on him. Let's just say the cocktail glasses had been refilled for a number of us at the table and leave it at that.

Hart leaned back and said, in so many words: "I've listened all night to what we can do for the *Dallas Morning News*. Well, let me tell you what the *Dallas Morning News* has done for me. They took a beat writer (Evan Grant) and made him a columnist so he could shove it up my ass every day. Then when he failed as a columnist, they put him back on the beat and now they expect me to return his calls every day after reading him shove it up my ass all last year. That's what they've done for me."

Twelve grown men were suddenly silent. I could almost hear the air rushing out of Hicks next to me as he puffed out his cheeks and saw his pleasant evening going up in smoke. Buck simply recalls a lot of jaws hitting the floor, including his own.

Having been emboldened by Grey Goose, I actually spoke up and said, "Well, your characterization of Evan as a failed columnist isn't exactly what happened."

In fairness, Hart wasn't entirely wrong about his characterization of the situation. A newspaper shifting someone from a reporting job into an outspoken columnist role and then back into a reporting gig is risking trouble.

However, I think everyone involved on the Rangers' side that night — this was, after all, their idea—would like to have seen Hart air his complaints in a more diplomatic fashion.

The dinner party ended shortly thereafter. The various participants went to their cars and headed home.

I close with this story for the simple reason that the night went the way that gatherings almost inevitably do when there's no lid on the bottle. The Rangers wanted to see what they could do to mend fences with us. The newspaper wanted to understand why a club's lack of cooperation from the owner, the GM, and sometimes the manager had reached such a level, and what we could do to fix it.

At the end we all left the Hicks mansion with the same thoughts in mind.

There were good intentions. But there was a lot of drinking. And it turned ugly and personal at the end.

EPILOGUE

"Loneliness has followed me my whole life. In cars. In
bars. There's no escape. I'm God's lonely man."

—Travis Bickle, *Taxi Driver*

IT'S THE NIGHT before Super Bowl 47. I hate Roman
numerals so let's just call it what it is, the 47th Super Bowl
played. Way back in Chapter One, the Ravens going to their
first Super Bowl was part of this story. Now they are preparing to play their second here in New Orleans against the San
Francisco 49ers.

I have written all I care to write about the game, about
two young quarterbacks making their first Super Bowl appearances, about Ray Lewis and deer antler spray and the end
of his long, troubled and yet inspiring (for some) journey. It is
the night before the game.

I am told New Orleans has more restaurants now than it
had before Katrina. I don't know if this is true but it certainly
looks to be the case from my hotel near the Convention

Center where there are three or four on every block no matter which direction you turn.

It is just past dusk on Saturday, not quite 24 hours before kickoff. The fans, the media, the thousands who have gathered in this crazy place are heading out for dinner, for drinks, for one last night of revelry. Like the players, I'm staying in.

In their case, it's all about saving energy. In mine, I am bored with going out. Had a great meal at a place called Cochon, a short walk from the hotel with David Moore (remember the *Morning News* writer I left stranded on the golf course when I was in jail?) and Buck Harvey of the *San Antonio Express-News* Tuesday night. Had another terrific meal with Woody and Plaschke at K-Paul on Thursday night. That was enough for me.

This whole "quitting drinking" thing comes with a price, although it's one well worth paying for many of us. Going to crowded restaurants where you have a 45-minute wait at the bar before you even get started with that two-hour meal— with rare, rare exceptions, that just doesn't appeal to me. I don't like being bored and lonely more than anyone else, but I'd rather stay in and eat by myself when I'm on the road than endure those long evenings of sipping Diet Cokes while others move from beer to wine or vodka.

It's nights like these that make me wish I could go back and try again. Take a drinking mulligan. Just give me one more shot at this thing and let me see if I can't keep it all under control this time around.

I don't have these thoughts very often. I know they aren't real. I know what I became when I started drinking at

16 and allowed the drinks to flow on an almost nightly basis until I was 54. I know that, in reality, the drinking gods gave me plenty of mulligans and I kept hooking it out of bounds time after time.

For years, I couldn't wait for these moments, the sun finally dipping down beyond the horizon. I told you earlier I was never really a daytime drinker. I waited with a reasonable degree of patience for nighttime to come. And back then I couldn't imagine anything better than a week in New Orleans for the Super Bowl.

I drove down to Houston for my first Super Bowl when I was home from the University of Colorado for Christmas. Getting tickets wasn't so difficult or costly then. Dolphins 24, Vikings 7. A totally unmemorable game. Bob Griese was 6-for-7—not on the opening drive but for the entire day as he handed off to Larry Csonka and Jim Kiick and Mercury Morris 51 times.

As a professional journalist I have been to 23 Super Bowls. My first was right here after the '85 season. The Super Bowl-shuffling Bears against the hopelessly overmatched Patriots. Jim McMahon sparring the with the media after mooning a TV helicopter at practice—New England Coach Ray Berry looking at his watch during a press conference, so, so anxious to get away from us and get the execution over with—playing pickup basketball and meeting Chicago sportswriter Rick Telander, who had written one of the books that inspired me to get into this business, *Heaven Is a Playground*, and making a friendship that continues to this day—nights on Bourbon Street, getting mistaken for Gary Fencik by fans one night at Pat O'Brien's—getting wasted in the Old Absinthe House, drinking some special concoction there that had the late, great Frank Luksa telling me, "Son, you might as well drink jet fuel."

I loved every minute of it.

This week has ranked considerably lower on the fun meter. That's fine. No one ever said life at 30 and life at 57 are supposed to be one and the same.

Life is still good. In fact, it's better than good.

My daughter, Rachel, is three months away from graduating from the University of Missouri. Part of me hates that she's graduating. I love those drives up to Columbia to go to football games with her, to meet her sorority sisters and eat pizza at Shakespeare's and burgers at Booches. I don't want her to age and be an adult with a job. I want her to be a fun-loving college kid, but, hey, I understand how this thing works.

My son, Ben, graduates high school in June. He's the only kid in America to narrow his college choices to Texas Tech and George Mason. If I can ever get him to do something like read a book from start to finish, he can be as good a writer as he wants to be regardless of which school he chooses. The stuff he cranks out on his blog about the Rangers or politics is better than what I wrote at the end of my *Daily Texan* days at UT.

My life is good. It is most decidedly not wild and not crazy. It is just as Mary Elizabeth Winstead said in *Smashed*, a movie not many of you bothered to see. You don't have to have a drinking problem to enjoy it. If you do have one and you have wrestled with it and you are winning (for now), then you will simply understand it that much better.

"My life is really different than it was," she tells her AA group. "I live alone. I'm bored a lot more. I'm really grateful for this boring life of mine."

I said I wouldn't get preachy in this book until the very end. Here we go and, don't worry, it will be quick.

I have been asked by more than one friend and media colleague this question: How do you know if you have a drinking problem?

There's a simple answer. If you ask that question, then chances are that you do. It's not necessarily something that requires a month at Betty Ford or regular AA visits to fix. It may not be as severe as my problem, either.

But unless you spend an inordinate amount of time thinking about problems that you clearly *don't* have, then your curiosity about your drinking begs at least some further examination.

As a society that has come to terms with other serious subjects, we spend far more time joking about drinking and getting drunk than we should. I've still never heard this conversation between two college age kids or young adults:

"What you got planned for tonight?"

"Oh, I don't know, think I'm going to go out and try to tear up my ACL or maybe sever my Achilles tendon."

"Great."

But I have heard this one my entire life:

"What you got planned for tonight?"

"Oh, I don't know, just go out and destroy a few brain cells."

"Cool."

* * *

In an age in which we have learned to take concussions in sports very seriously—no one simply shrugs off "getting their bell rung" any more—we still make jokes about drinking enough alcohol to do significant brain damage.

Apparently, the fact that you don't register the damage right away (unless you land on your head and tear it open like I did) makes it acceptable.

It's crazy. And, to me, anyway, those jokes, those cliché lines that appear in virtually every show you can think of— *"ohh, what a day, boy, I need a drink"*—they stopped generating laughs years ago.

All I can tell you is that there's a life out there, an adult life, without drinking that's very different but incredibly rewarding as well.

My life isn't what the fans on the streets of New Orleans here think it is. They shouted at me today as they stumbled past under what appeared to be a noose of beads. They shouted at me from cars. Some of them even got it right, yelling "Hey, *Around the Horn*" instead of "Hey, *PTI.*"

Some of them still want to buy me shots. Saying no is not difficult. It's not uncomfortable. I know what I am and what I'm not any more.

And, hey, what if I am wrong about this entire premise? What if I'm no longer in any danger of having a seizure and I could go back to being a drinker, maybe even master that "just a couple of glasses of wine with dinner" approach that was so elusive?

It's OK. I'll stick with the words of our show's tremendously supportive host, Tony Reali, who has the occasional cocktail but isn't much of a drinker. He congratulated me when I concluded my second year of sobriety, saying, "You're not missing a damn thing."

Someone else wears the crown as life of the party. My kids, my parents and my liver are eternally grateful.

ACKNOWLEDGEMENTS

In 2009, my first agent, Brian Wood, did a remarkable but impossible job trying to sell this book when it was little more than a title and an arrest report. I stopped writing it for nearly a year and went a different route when I got back to it, but I thank Brian for helping me begin this project.

My support at Vigliano Associates has been exceptional, and that's especially true of Hilary Mau, who has tirelessly answered the hundreds of questions that I posed both before and after the book became reality. Cary Goldstein of Twelve Publishing supplied me with support and confidence, even after choosing not to pursue the book.

Messages and calls from Mark Kriegel, who writes the kind of sports biographies I can only read, not produce on my own, gave me confidence to keep going although I'm not sure he's even aware of it. Praise and/or advice from authors as gifted as Jon Wertheim and Peter Richmond remains beyond my comprehension.

Thanks to Buz, who continues to do great, meaningful work in helping people turn their lives around after they have found their way to jail. He was more helpful to me than he will ever know.

Thanks to Dr. Bruce Mickey who played an important role not just in removing the stitches from my head and prescribing a course for recovery but also in pouring through the hundreds of pages of my hospital records to uncover the information I could never decipher on my own. And the most important thing he did as I was leaving his office in 2011 was saying, "I want you to write this, stick with it."

In addition, I should thank all the emergency room personnel, physicians, nurses and administrators at both Parkland and UT-Southwestern Medical Center who made my "visits" there the first steps in my personal recovery. I also appreciate the hundreds of pages of medical records they supplied me as I tried to figure out exactly what in the world was happening with me in 2008 and 2009.

Mostly I want to thank all the people I don't know and will probably never meet who have e-mailed me or contacted me on twitter the last few years regarding my drinking problems or, in some cases, to discuss their own. These people are the reason I wrote this book.

Finally I want to thank Willis Ray Cowlishaw, who hopefully has not wasted one minute of his life thinking that the drinking problems that sent him to AA, which produced an even more wonderful life for him, had anything to do with my own issues. The hereditary stuff people tell you is bullshit.

My drinking problems are my own, and if I'm beating them, you have only helped me find the proper course (fairway, so to speak) and I love you for it.

ABOUT THE AUTHOR

Tim Cowlishaw has been *The Dallas Morning News'* lead sports columnist since July 1988, and has won APSE's Best Sports Columnist in Texas four times. He has been a regular panelist on the ESPN sports talk show *Around the Horn* since its debut in November 2002, and has also worked with ESPN as lead reporter for the network's *NASCAR Now* coverage from 2007-08.

Prior to *The Dallas Morning News* and *Around the Horn*, Tim covered the Dallas Cowboys for six seasons and the Dallas Stars for three. He also covered the Rangers as backup beat writer, the Oklahoma Sooners' football, and was the *San Jose Mercury News'* beat writer on the San Francisco Giants.

Tim attended the University of Texas at Austin, and has two children, Rachel and Ben.

CPSIA information can be obtained at www.ICGtesting.com
Printed in the USA
LVOW061256100613

337703LV00002B/2/P